Children's
Both

CN00867778

The Boy Who Disappeared and Other Stories

The Boy Who Disappeared and Other Stories

ROB KEELEY

Copyright © 2023 Rob Keeley

The moral right of the author has been asserted.

Apart from any fair dealing for the purposes of research or private study,
or criticism or review, as permitted under the Copyright, Designs and Patents
Act 1988, this publication may only be reproduced, stored or transmitted, in
any form or by any means, with the prior permission in writing of the
publishers, or in the case of reprographic reproduction in accordance with
the terms of licences issued by the Copyright Licensing Agency. Enquiries
concerning reproduction outside those terms should be sent to the publishers.

This is a work of fiction. Names, characters, businesses, places, events
and incidents are either the products of the author's imagination
or used in a fictitious manner. Any resemblance to actual persons,
living or dead, or actual events is purely coincidental.

Matador
Unit E2 Airfield Business Park,
Harrison Road, Market Harborough,
Leicestershire. LE16 7UL
Tel: 0116 2792299
Email: books@troubador.co.uk
Web: www.troubador.co.uk/matador
Twitter: @matadorbooks

ISBN 978 1803136 448

British Library Cataloguing in Publication Data.
A catalogue record for this book is available from the British Library.

Printed and bound in the UK by TJ Books Limited, Padstow, Cornwall
Typeset in 11pt Book Antiqua by Troubador Publishing Ltd, Leicester, UK

Matador is an imprint of Troubador Publishing Ltd

For Martin

Contents

The Boy Who Disappeared

"Now, Year Six, we're very pleased to meet someone new. Ellis has come all the way from Leicester. So let's give him a big welcome to our class."

Isla looked at Ellis. He was a big, stocky, red-faced boy, with dark brown hair and a green jumper that wasn't quite the school sweater. He didn't speak, and looked rather solemn. She felt sorry for him, coming into a new school, knowing no one. She made a space for him next to her.

It was only when they were doing English that things began to happen. Ellis was quietly doing his work, when Isla felt something go:

flick!

at her ponytail.

Isla washed her hair every day. She had seven hairbands, all the same. She hated anyone else touching her hair.

She looked at the window. It wasn't open very far in February, but maybe there was a draught.

She worked on. Then she felt a *flick!* again.

It was him, she was sure. He was staring down at his book, and his big red hands were on the table. But a minute later, when she stopped watching… *flick!*

She gave Ellis a look.

A big, cheeky grin spread across his face.

At lunchtime, he was there again, just behind her in the queue. There was one shortbread biscuit left, with icing and sprinkles on the top, just the way Isla liked it. She was next in line, and it was hers.

She took one glance towards the drinks.

Then she looked back, and the biscuit had gone.

She turned to see Ellis, munching and smirking.

The dinner lady hadn't noticed. No one seemed to notice Ellis.

They did Technology in the afternoon, and nothing else happened. But she saw Ellis grinning at her.

At home, the TV news was gloomy.

"There are two cases in the UK, but it's under control. It's just like the flu. We'll be fine, as long as we wash our hands…"

Isla washed hers a lot, and sang the birthday song to herself. She had no sisters or brothers.

The next morning, Ellis was getting worse. Isla's ponytail was still within easy reach, and she felt him going *flick, flick, flick*, all the way through Algebra. Isla was starting to go as red as he was. He was going to suffer for this…

Then came the pencil sharpener. It was a very fancy one, which Isla had bought in the gift shop at the airport. It was covered with little flags, and played three different National Anthems. Everyone needed Isla's special permission to use it.

It was on the table in front of her during Geography,

and then it wasn't. Isla searched her pencil case, her bag, all her pockets, so there could be no mistake.

She knew it was him, but she couldn't prove it, and she wasn't going to snitch on a new boy.

She looked darkly at him. His big, brown eyes were full of mischief.

He was doing things for the rest of that day, sliding her chair away when she was about to sit down, moving her bookmark to the other end of the book, poking at her pencil case until he nearly broke the zip. Those hands of his never kept still.

Finally, at the end of the day, Mrs Lee was making announcements, when Isla felt one enormous:

flick!

and she kicked out, under the table, and hit Mikele by mistake. Mikele gave a massive scream, and clutched her ankle, and Isla got sent to Mrs Conteh's office.

She went home, boiling with rage.

That boy… that boy… that boy…

Then suddenly, the lockdown came, and he wasn't there anymore. And neither was school. Isla found herself having lessons in the living room, talking to Mrs Lee online.

She enjoyed it, for the first few days. It was nice and quiet. No stupid boys taking her stuff or messing with her hair. She went on with her Maths and English, and did P.E. with Joe. It was quiet… it really was very quiet.

This couldn't be for long? They only had a few months left. This virus was killing the rest of their time at primary school. She asked Mrs Lee, but even she didn't know.

"We'll just have to wait and see."

Isla watched every bulletin.

"Fourteen more cases. Three more deaths. But we're going to get through this! We're here for you. Don't panic buy, work from home, support bubbles, blah blah blah…"

Isla didn't think *anyone* knew what was happening.

Mum and Dad were both furloughed, and it was weird, having them at home all day. All the food was being delivered, and Mum said they had to watch the bills. Isla phoned a few people from school, had video calls with Nan, but felt oddly that there was something missing.

One day, she felt the draught blow her hair. Maybe Ellis's ghost was here, giving her ponytail a phantom flick.

She wondered what he was doing. Were his parents working? What was he having for breakfast? Was he doing his work? Was he using her pencil sharpener? Would she ever see him again?

Why did she even care?

She would have quite liked to get in touch. Just to see how he was. But she didn't know how.

She had never even talked to him…

Then the end of the summer term neared, and they were back at school! But not real school. Socially-distanced school. There was striped tape on the floors, and everyone spent even more time washing their hands. Isla wondered if she were still asleep at home, dreaming about school, because nothing seemed real.

Ellis was there, in the same old scruffy green jumper. When Isla sat down, two metres from him, he gave her a grin. He couldn't do anything, because he couldn't come near. She still hated him, like she hated all boys, but at least they were able to talk. His Dad was out of work now. His Mum was a hairdresser – that made sense! – worried about how her business would keep going. His eyes still looked wicked. She could see he was longing to mess with her hair. She gave him a warning glare.

Then it was the end of term, with a farewell outdoor Assembly and a burger and fries, and their time at primary school was over. Isla felt she'd been robbed. Someone had stolen part of her childhood.

Then September came, and it was time for secondary school. This year had turned into a rollercoaster. Isla felt very smart and grown-up in her dark blue blazer and trousers, yet she felt she was too young to be here. She knew a few people from her old school, but none of them was in her form. Everyone was still seated apart. She felt there was a big space beside her, where someone should be. She kept thinking somebody had flicked her hair, yet when she looked round, there was no one there.

One evening, she felt very alone and afraid, and rang five different people from her old class, trying to find a way to contact Ellis. In the end, she got his landline number. But still she didn't call.

What was wrong with her? She hated him... didn't she?

The next evening, Nan came on for a video chat, and Isla told her the whole story. Nan just smiled, and said:

"Oh, Isla. Why *do* boys show off, in front of girls?"

Isla went straight off and rang the number.

She talked a lot more to Ellis after that, on the phone and on video, with his big tomato face filling her screen. He was at a boys-only school, and hating it. His Dad was still jobless. His big brother Tyrone had started work at a new supermarket...

Then, in the New Year, someone very clever found a vaccine, and life began to return to normal. People were finally able to meet again, and Isla rang Ellis and asked him round for tea.

He came, in a black tracksuit over a football shirt, with a cheap signet ring, gleaming white trainers and no socks. Isla thought it must be his best suit. It was the first time they'd met since last summer. He said:

"Miss me, did you?"

and grinned all over his stupid face when Isla blushed.

He ate two plates of chicken and rice, and three chocolate cake bars, and pinched the only orange one before she could get it, and burped loudly, and kept defeating her on the games console, and fiddled with her DJ robot and broke it, and was just as annoying as he had been last year.

Finally, he said:

"Missed you too."

and slapped his hand down on her palm, as if doing a low-five.

When he took it away, Isla saw her pencil sharpener there.

They sat watching TV together. There was nothing about the virus now.

Then Isla felt him go:

Flick!

This story was written in late 2020

Hold The Front Page

"So, this book review of yours, Oscar." Mrs Hoyle picked up a single sheet of paper from her desk. "There are one or two questions I'd like to ask you about it."

Standing in front of the teacher's desk, Oscar was shuffling his feet, continuing a hole in the carpet which many other pupils had started.

He looked at the paper. He'd written the review quickly, on the morning it was due to be handed in, and his handwriting wasn't his best. It looked as if a centipede had taken a bath in some ink before going for a walk across the paper.

"For "genre" you've written "book". I was hoping for a bit more detail, Oscar." Mrs Hoyle picked the book up from alongside the review. "Then there's "What happens?" where you've written something oddly like the blurb printed on the back of the book. Only shorter."

Oscar looked at the floor.

"For "What did you think of it?"" Mrs Hoyle went on, "you've written "Very good". And for "What was your favourite part?" you've written "All of it"."

Her voice was growing louder, and kids at a nearby table were grinning. Selina aimed a very superior smile in Oscar's direction. Her review had got a gold star and was already up on the wall. Oscar couldn't scowl at her without Mrs Hoyle seeing.

"But the most interesting part," Mrs Hoyle said, "is where you were asked your favourite character and you've written "Sam". When asked why, you've put: "He was very funny." Do you still think that, Oscar?"

Oscar shrugged. "Yeah."

"Well, that's interesting. Because the Sam in the book… is actually a girl. Samantha. And she betrays her whole family and gets them arrested by the Secret Police. While the planet Earth lies in ruins. You found that hilarious, did you, Oscar?"

Oscar said nothing. But he could still see Selina smiling.

"Correct me if I'm wrong, but I don't think you've actually read this book?" Mrs Hoyle handed the book to Oscar. "Now, I want you to take this home tonight, and instead of watching TV or going on the Internet or whatever you young people do these days, I want you to read. And I want to see a review of what you've read, first thing tomorrow. At least three chapters, Oscar. All right? And you can take the book back to the library when you've finished."

"Yes, miss."

Oscar's day had started badly and, like many school days, slowly got worse. At lunchtime they were on last dinners and there was nothing left except salmon nuggets, which Oscar hated. He had to sit next to Selina all through Art, and see her smiling at him. He knew she was thinking about the book review.

Then, when the end of the day finally came, Oscar got home to find his younger sister Maisie had borrowed his football again.

"Everyone knows girls are the *best* footballers," she had told Oscar. "I'm going to start a team, with Billie and Olivia. We only need eight more people now."

Oscar shoved a pile of football magazines off his desk and onto the floor. There was a stain under the desk where he'd once spilt a glass of cola.

He looked at the library book. Review? He felt like writing a review, all right, but not of the book.

Without bothering to take his coat off, he sat down, ripped a piece of paper from a writing pad and picked up his pen.

My name is Oscar. From Heather Class. And this is a review of my life. It stinks.

He was enjoying this. He went on.

Mrs Hoyle my teacher is a rotten mean old bag. Selina is a show-off who dies her hare. And my sister Maisie can't kick a ball strate.

He was feeling better by the minute. He continued writing.

The school dinners taste like cardbord and there's never nothing nice left. I hate our school and I want to run away and join a football team. Mite learn more.

As for my Mum –

He jumped, as he saw his bedroom door opening. He just had time to shove the piece of paper out of sight, inside the front cover of the library book, before his Mum appeared.

"What are you doing, Oscar?"

"Homework," Oscar said. "Mrs Hoyle liked my book review so much, she wants me to write another one."

"Hmm." His mother looked around the room, at the clothing scattered everywhere, the pile of forgotten toys toppling over in the corner. "Well, finish your work first. But then get this room tidied up. You can have your tea when you've finished. And take your coat off in the house!"

"OK." Oscar looked down at the desk.

As soon as she'd gone, he picked up the book again. He supposed he had to read it. Why couldn't they have made it into a movie? He'd got away with doing two book reviews that way. The story was usually nearly the same.

He opened the first chapter.

By the time Oscar had read and written and tidied, he was ready for his tea. He didn't bother to wait for

Maisie, who was footballing on the green at the end of the road. He was so hungry that he even felt ready for Mum's tuna bake. Afterwards, he watched some TV and went to bed.

First thing the following morning, he went to the school library and put the book back on the shelf. Then he handed the book review in to Mrs Hoyle.

It wasn't a bad book. But he was glad to see the back of it.

It was only halfway through Assembly that he realised what was in the front of it.

Oscar sat and panicked all through Maths.

He'd searched his schoolbag. The writing pad was there, but the review of his life wasn't. He remembered shoving it inside the library book before Mum came in. After that…

It was still inside the front cover. A piece of paper, with his name and his class on it, saying exactly what he thought about the school… and Selina… and what had he said about Mrs Hoyle? Something old bag? He couldn't even remember.

It was morning break before he got the chance to go back to the library. There were a couple of girls from Juniper Class on library duty.

"Kimberley!" Oscar ran up to the desk. "Can I have my book back? There's a bit I want to read again."

Kimberley pushed a pink card over. "Write the full details on there, please. Book title, author name, ISBN…"

"What's an ISBN?" Oscar shook his head. "I can tell you what it was called –"

"Just write it on there," Kimberley said. "It's a system. We made it up ourselves. It's to save time."

Muttering furiously, Oscar took a pen and scribbled the book title on the card. He couldn't remember the author's name.

"Oh." Kimberley took the card. "That's a fiction book, isn't it? Pink card is for non-fiction. Give him a blue card, Sophie."

Sophie handed another card over.

"But…" Oscar stared at it. "I've already…"

He met their gaze. He wrote the title out again.

He looked at the clock on the wall. It was nearly the end of break.

"Thank you." Kimberley took the blue card. "Now cross-reference, please, Sophie. Then leave the card in the box for Mrs Cole to put onto the database."

Sophie took the card and checked it against some sheets of paper on a clipboard. There seemed to be about five thousand pages for her to look through.

"Juniper Reference… 93…" Sophie looked at Oscar. "Ah yes. It's out with another reader. Went five minutes ago."

"Couldn't you have told me that before?" Oscar yelled.

Kimberley pointed to a notice on the desk in front of her. It said: *Quiet Please*.

"Selina's got it," Sophie said. "Would you like to read a book about dinosaurs instead, Oscar? Oscar…?"

Oscar went out very quickly into the yard. The bell would be going at any moment.

If Selina saw that piece of paper…

He found her showing off her new solar-powered watch to two of the other girls from their class. When she saw him she looked at him as usual. As if she'd like to step on him. But not as if she'd like to murder him. So she couldn't have found the piece of paper yet.

"What do *you* want?"

"Selina…" Oscar forced himself to smile. "Sophie said you've got the book I took back to the library… can I borrow it off you, please? Just quickly?"

"Didn't know you could read," Selina said. The other girls laughed. Selina turned to them. "And they wonder why girls do better at school than boys. Don't think he's ever read anything that's not a football magazine. He was probably surprised to find it had a story. Probably thought you could only have eleven characters and two reserves."

Oscar bit his tongue.

"What do you want it for?" Selina went on. "You've done the review. You were lucky to get away with only three chapters."

"I…" Oscar swallowed. "I want to check the author's name. Might buy it."

"He's *buying* books, now!" Selina shrilled. "TV must have broken." She smirked. "Anyway, I haven't got it. I've given it to Mrs Cole. It's in her classroom."

Oscar turned a peculiar shade of green.

"For Book Club. I read some of it in the library last

week, looked good. So I suggested she could read it to us at Book Club. She was very grateful. She does rely on me a lot, you know."

Oscar staggered away.

"Yes, of course, Oscar." Mrs Cole smiled. "I'd be very pleased for you to join our Book Club. I'm glad to see you boys interested in something other than football or cars. But I have to admit, I'm surprised. I suppose it's all the extra reading practice you've done with Mrs Hoyle?"

"Yeah," Oscar said. His lips were dry. His throat felt like the inside of a vacuum cleaner. He could see the book, sitting on Mrs Cole's desk. The front cover was slightly open. "I'm really into books now, and like, reading, and words, and stuff. And dystopian visions of a future Earth." He remembered that one from the back of the book.

"Well, good for you." Mrs Cole gave him a cheap plastic badge from a box on her desk. It said: *I Love A Good Book*. "There's your badge. The club takes place every two weeks. We meet in here on Friday afternoons, after school."

You would, Oscar thought. He stared longingly at the book. "Selina said we were reading that, miss. Could I just…" He stretched out a hand towards it.

"Not just at the moment, Oscar." Mrs Cole picked up the book. "I've got to make some worksheets based on it. It looks good though, doesn't it? I'll be reading the first chapter to you all tomorrow. Looks like the sort of book that could bring quite a lot of surprises." She put it into her bag.

"Yeah, miss…" Oscar muttered. "Think it would."

In the middle of the night, all the things he had written came back to Oscar. The words flew around his mind.

Selina is a show-off who dyes her hair.

The school dinners taste like cardboard.

Mrs Hoyle my teacher is a rotten mean old bag.

He was sweating, yet his insides felt cold. Suppose Mrs Cole had already found the piece of paper? Suppose Selina had… no, they'd be scraping him off the walls by now if she had. But what if Mrs Cole took it to Mrs Raeburn, the Head? Or suppose Mrs Cole found it and read it out at Book Club, in front of everybody?

"One more bit of trouble at that school," Oscar's Dad had said the week before, "and you can forget about going to Florida for our holidays. I've had just about enough of this, Oscar."

When Oscar finally fell asleep, he dreamed that the Secret Police had come for him, and marched him through the ruined and burning streets of the town for trial, just like in the book. They threw him into a courtroom. Watching, and hissing, and glaring at him were Kimberley, Sophie and a boy he'd met on holiday last year.

Facing him, in red robes and a long white wig, was the judge. She pushed the wig back from her face. And Oscar saw that it was Selina.

She was holding Oscar's review.

"The prisoner, Oscar," her voice boomed and resounded from the walls, "has been found guilty of insulting my hairstyle and being very rude to teachers. There is no penalty great enough for such crimes."

Oscar tried to speak, but he couldn't open his mouth. Selina's solar-powered watch had grown to enormous size and was wrapped around his face, ticking deafeningly in his ears.

"Oscar, you will be imprisoned for all eternity in a cellar full of rats. And you will spend the time breaking up rocks to build a new school library. You will have nothing to eat but salmon nuggets and tuna bake. Take him down."

Oscar tried desperately to speak. He turned to the Secret Police officer by his side.

It was Mrs Hoyle.

"Down!" Selina reached and pulled a huge red lever that had suddenly appeared beside her. "DOWN! DOWN! DOWN!"

Oscar felt a trapdoor give way beneath his feet. He was falling… falling…

"AAAAAAAAAARGGGGGGGGGHHHHHHHH!"

He woke up to find he'd fallen out of bed.

Oscar was told off three times the next day for not listening.

He was expecting at any moment to be sent to Mrs Raeburn, or Mrs Hoyle to call him out to the front, or Mrs Cole to come in holding the piece of paper.

Surely Mrs Cole must have found it? If she'd been reading the book?

At three-fifteen, he was longing to join the other boys hurtling towards the gate, but instead he went to Mrs Cole's classroom for Book Club.

He was horrified to find the only empty chair was next to Selina. She looked at him as normal, as if he were something she'd found stuck to her shoe. But at least she wasn't in cellar of rats mode yet.

He made sure she didn't have a lever anywhere near her.

"Now," Mrs Cole said. "I've found something very interesting I'd like to read to you."

She opened the book and removed an object.

The room went black, and Oscar grabbed something for support. It turned out to be Selina's arm. She gave him a furious glare.

Slowly, Oscar forced himself to look at what Mrs Cole was holding.

It was a bookmark. He started breathing again.

He could see right into the front of the book now. There was nothing inside the front cover. She must have found it! So – why wasn't he in trouble? Or... He tried to remember. Had he stuck it further inside the book? Maybe it was in the middle pages? Or at the back? He was sure it was the front.

Oh no! Suppose it had fallen out in this classroom somewhere? Or in Mrs Cole's bag? Or somewhere in school – not the staffroom...

"The greatest day of Sam's life..." Mrs Cole started to

read, "*was when she knew her moment had come. She stood before the Junior Council and said*, Oscar what are you doing?"

Everyone tittered. Oscar was leaning over to take a look under Mrs Cole's desk and was almost on the floor.

"Miss." Selina was looking embarrassed. "Can I sit somewhere else, please?"

"If you can't behave, Oscar," Mrs Cole said, "then I shall ask you to leave this Book Club and go straight home. Shall we continue?"

Oscar didn't hear another word Mrs Cole said, for the whole hour.

Where was his review?

At the end of the club, Mrs Cole made a final announcement.

"As most of you will know, today is when we start putting you into Reading Pairs. Before we meet again in a fortnight, please would you get together with the person sitting next to you…"

Oscar and Selina exchanged horrified glances.

"And read a book of your choice. Then, in two weeks I'd like you to do a little presentation on what you thought of the book."

"Why do I have to be with *you*?" Selina asked, as the club broke up. "Anyway, it'll be an easy job, if we do this one. I've read nearly the whole thing already."

She reached into her schoolbag and produced another copy of the library book.

Oscar let out a yelp. Gathering her things together, Mrs Cole gave him a look.

"Where did that come from?"

"The library, muttonhead." Selina put on her coat, with its fake fur collar. "They've got two of them. I decided I couldn't wait for us to finish it here, so I got the other one out this afternoon." She turned to Mrs Cole. "We can do this book, can't we, miss? As long as we don't give the ending away?"

She looked back to see Oscar trying to peer inside the cover.

"Will you get your great spotty schnozzle out of my book?"

She was heading for the door.

"Selina!" Oscar ran after her. He took a deep breath. What he was about to do required all his courage. "Are you doing anything tonight?"

He winced, as two passing boys went: "Whoooo!"

"Why?" Selina didn't bother to look at Oscar as she moved towards the junior exit.

"We…" Oscar caught his breath. "We could do the book thing tonight. The presentation. I could come and have tea with you…"

Selina stared at him.

"Well, for utter nerve you win the International Award. I suppose so. As my bassoon tutor's got flu."

She turned and faced Oscar.

"You do exactly as I say, you don't mess about with my bookshelf, you eat nicely, you wipe your feet and you don't take your shoes off. OK?"

Oscar threw aside what was left of his pride. "OK."

The evening that followed was one of the longest of Oscar's life. After calling home to explain what he was doing, at which his Mum looked oddly relieved, he walked to Selina's house. The room that she called her "den" could have held a disco for fifty kids, and the carpet was bright pink. There were posters of girl bands on those walls which weren't already filled with Selina's certificates. She seemed to have done everything. Pony Club Champion. Welsh Harp. Creative Cookery.

Oscar was made to hold large pieces of paper while Selina wrote their book presentation on them in smelly marker pen. His only break was when they went into what Selina called the "dining area" for tea. Tuna bake, again. Selina spent the whole meal criticising his hair… and the state of his shoes… and his table manners…

He was only putting himself through this to get a chance of searching the book, but she never let go of it, nor left him alone with it once.

He was going hot and cold. At any moment, she might find…

Thankfully, she was looking mostly at the later chapters.

"We'll finish off next week," she said finally. "I don't expect you to read it, you'll take too long. When we go to Book Club you can just hold the sheets up for me. Think you can manage that?"

The doorbell rang.

"I'd better get that. Mum's gone to Meditation class."
She left the room.

Oscar made a run for the book. He grabbed it, stuck his hand beneath the front cover, then the back cover. He flicked right through the pages, then turned the book upside down and shook it.

Nothing!

"It was the lady for Mum's collecting box." Selina re-entered. "What *are* you doing to that book?"

Oscar turned to her. He flicked through the pages one more time.

"There we go. Last page. Didn't take me long to finish it, after all."

He threw it down on the pink rug.

"And now I'm going home."

Oscar walked home in a daze.

He'd seen inside both copies now. Where was the review?

It must have fallen out. So either it was floating around school somewhere… or it was in Selina's house.

Either way, he'd had it.

He went into his room, where all this trouble had started. He knew the review wasn't there. He'd searched from top to bottom the night before. Even had the mattress off the bed.

He looked round as he saw Maisie standing in the doorway.

"I brought your football back," she said. "We'll buy our own, soon."

She placed the football on the desk. Then she reached into her pocket.

"Is this yours? Thought it was your writing."

Oscar's eyes bulged.

Maisie was holding his review.

"I found it when I brought the ball back, day before yesterday. You were having your tea – you know, it's rude not to wait for other people. I thought the book looked good, then I found this in the front. I *can* kick a ball straight, by the way."

Oscar's mouth was opening and closing like a goldfish.

"All the girls at Brownies thought it was funny last night, too. Apart from the bit about me, of course. But don't worry. They won't tell Mrs Hoyle."

She folded the review and put it back into her pocket.

She pushed into the room and sat at Oscar's desk. She took a chocolate bar from his secret drawer.

"And now… there's something I'd like you to do for me."

Guess What?

"Miss! Miss! MISS!"

"What have you done now, Toby? Oh, now look at that mess! Look, egg all over the floor! Don't tread it around, Toby, just keep still! Now, what happened?"

"Well, I was whisking really hard, and I didn't see the box –"

"Honestly, Toby, you know there was only one egg each. Now, let's find some kitchen roll."

"Can you make these cakes without egg, miss?"

"No, Toby. We'll have to see if anyone else can spare you one. Be careful, everyone, there's egg on the floor."

"We've got to make them, miss, it's for charity!"

"Yes, all right, Toby. Really… I don't know why we do these sponsored bakes. We could have done another sponsored silence."

"That's not as much fun, miss."

"It is for me, Toby. All right everyone, the rest of you can move over to the baking trays when you're ready."

*

"Hello? Hi, Tommo? Yeah, it's me, Garth. Yeah, I know you're only on the other side of the climbing frame – yeah, I can see you. Hello! But I want to test my new phone out. Hey, we had a right laugh in the sponsored bake. Toby went and broke his egg! There was stuff everywhere."

*

"Hey, Kitty, have you heard? Toby. In the sponsored bake. He broke his leg!"

"No! You're kidding!"

"No, they had to call an ambulance and everything. There was stuff all over the kitchen floor. Must have fallen."

"Poor Toby. Hear that, April? Tommo says Toby's broken his leg. There's an ambulance coming to school, and they've had to phone his Mum as well."

"Hey, it sounds like one of them adverts on TV. You can get loads of money for things like that, you know. It's called personal injury, or no-win-no-fee, or something. You can get money for hurting yourself, but you've only got three years to do it in."

"Well, I fell off the climbing frame once."

"When?"

"Year One."

"Ah, you're too late then. Should have waited 'til Juniors, then you could have been rich. You'll know, next time."

"Hey, d'you hear that, Belle? Toby's broken his leg falling on some cake mix, and his Mum and Dad are going to sue the school! We should go and see him."

*

"Could I have the haddock nuggets, please? And herby diced potatoes? Cheers. Hey, did you hear about Toby, Jenny? He's in hospital with a broken leg. There was cake mix all over the kitchen floor, and Toby fell."

"No!"

"Yeah! Paris sponge and custard, please. Toby and I are in Drama Club together. He won't be able to play the Ostrich now. You need both legs."

"Could I have cheese and an apple, please? I heard the whole class is getting the afternoon off to go and see him."

"When?"

"Today! They're going in the minibus, after lunch."

"Well, what about English? There's some of their class in our group. We're doing a play, and Toby's meant to be playing the Prince."

"Dunno. Hey, maybe they'll shut the whole group down for the day."

*

"Hear that, Belle? They're shutting the whole school down for the afternoon, and we're all going to see Toby."

"What, the whole school? In that children's ward? Yeah, right."

"No, they're doing it in Toby's honour! We all get the afternoon off."

"Nice one! Good old Tobes! Wish he'd break his leg more often. Hey, we could go to the amusement arcade, or the park, or do crazy golf. It's nicer weather today than you ever get at weekends."

"I heard there's an ambulance coming to school."

"No, the ambulance has been! Took Toby to hospital, didn't it?"

"No, someone said they're coming this afternoon. It's probably like when the Fire Brigade came, you know, they showed us how the hose worked and Mandy got to try a helmet on. Maybe this lot'll let us do bandages, or have a play with the oxygen."

"Well, they can't be giving us the afternoon off then, can they? Honestly, you'd believe anything. I reckon they should just give Toby some space."

*

"Hey, you'll never guess what? Toby, in Lime Class. He's going into space!"

"NO!"

"He is! With oxygen. 'Soon as his leg's better. It's a charity fundraising thing. They send you into space, and it helps to cure others."

"We've all got to sponsor him. It's like sponsored walks. Further he gets, the more you pay."

"Wonder if he'll get as far as Mars?"

"That'd be about a tenner, I should think. I've only got 50p. I'll say the Moon."

"I'll say the ionosphere. I'm saving up for a new bike."

"I heard he's going to play crazy golf up there. You know, like the astronauts played golf on the Moon?"

"You can play crazy golf for a few pounds down here. And the atmosphere's breathable."

"Thanks, Julian. Hey, what time's that ambulance getting here?"

"I thought it was the Fire Brigade again."

"No, police, I think."

"No, it's the Fire Brigade. And they're bringing all their ladders!"

*

"Lydia, you've been very helpful to me while Mrs Hoskins has been away, but are you *sure* the whole school's being evacuated?"

"The Fire Brigade's coming, miss. The cooker in the kitchen caught fire, or something, during the sponsored bake. And Toby's in hospital!"

"All right, everyone out into the yard while we find out what's going on."

*

"For the last time, everyone, you are *not* getting the afternoon off, the ambulance people are *not* coming, and *no one* is going into orbit. Although I may be, shortly, if you don't concentrate on your work. Now, Alicia, will you read the first poem, please?"

"Miss… There's another class outside the window.

With that supply teacher, Miss Thing. It's not P.E., is it? And Mrs Raeburn's going out. She doesn't look too pleased, does she?"

*

"Garth, it's Tommo. Over here, by the netball court! Hello. Listen, mate, are you *sure* Toby's broke his leg? I've just seen him playing football!"

"Might have known it was all garbage. I dunno who starts these daft rumours."

"Yeah, they want to get their facts right, don't they? You coming to Drama Club, tonight?"

*

"Yes, I've just dropped him at Drama Club. Did I tell you, he's playing the Camel? Well, one half. It's a very important part. Two humps."

"Lovely. Meanwhile, I've got to find something for their tea. You seen any special offers? I've got one decided she's vegetarian this week, one who won't eat cheese and another who doesn't like anything in breadcrumbs. There's not much left."

"There's some soya dinosaurs in aisle seventeen."

"Ah, thanks. Alfie came home and told me the maddest story. Apparently Toby got trapped in the kitchen during the sponsored bake, had to kick his way out! He hurt his leg doing it."

"I heard Toby was doing a charity parachute jump!

His leg can't be all that bad. *Hello!* How are *you*?"

"OK. Trying to find a birthday cake for Saturday that no one else has had. Hope your two are coming, are they? I've lost track of Alicia's invitations, and the balloon modeller's sprained his wrist. Nightmare. By the way, do you know what happened at the school this afternoon? There was some sort of false alarm. I was told half the school was evacuated, and either the Fire Brigade came, or Air-Sea Rescue, Alicia wasn't sure."

"Don't know why they wanted Air-Sea Rescue. The school's only got a pond."

"Probably a load of rubbish. I don't know why kids spread these silly stories."

"Hey, look! Look! No, don't look. It's her from the beauty parlour, you know, her with the nails? You'll never guess what…"

The Midnight Feast

"Liam!" Liam felt himself being shaken. "Liam!"

Liam woke up. He opened his eyes. Justin was standing over him.

"What?"

"It's quarter to twelve!" Justin went on.

Liam blinked. "Did you wake me up just to tell me that?"

"Don't you remember?" Justin went on. "It's time for the best bit. The midnight feast!"

Liam groaned.

He took a look across the back room of Justin's house. A shaft of moonlight lit the scene. Nearby, in their sleeping bags, lay Ben and Lucas. On the other side of the room was a heap of old DVDs and video games.

"I know we didn't get all the people we wanted," Justin said. "But I've organised the midnight feast, anyway. I mean, we always have a midnight feast at a sleepover."

"It's not a sleepover," Liam said. "Sleepovers are for girls. This is an indoor boot camp."

He passed his hand over his face. With only four of them here, it hardly seemed worth it. Midnight feasts always sounded like such fun when you were planning them. Once they arrived, Liam always felt he wanted sleep far more than food.

He caught Justin's eye.

"Yeah. All right. Sure." He looked around. No fourth sleeping bag was visible. "Where are *you* sleeping, then?"

"Upstairs," Justin said. "In my bedroom." He paused. "Well, it's my house."

"We're having a sleepover," Liam said. "I mean, boot camp. And you're sleeping *in your own bed*?"

He shook his head.

"Now, remember the rules," Justin said. "I will now confidentially give you the secret location." He leaned over and whispered in Liam's ear.

"Lewis's room?" Liam said loudly.

"Ssh!" Justin grabbed Liam's arm. "It's a secret!"

"Justin…" Liam said. "You're being very childish over this. After all, we're not kids anymore, you know." He paused. "You do remember the secret knock?"

"Yes," Justin said. "Dum-diddy-dum-diddy-dum-diddy-dum-dum…"

"No," Liam frowned. "Dum-diddy-dum-diddy-dum-dum-dum! Come on, J, get it right!"

He emerged, very slowly, from his sleeping bag. The room felt cold, and everything looked so spooky, all lit up. He wasn't hungry. And he still felt half-asleep.

But he wasn't going to admit it to Justin.

He stood up.

"Why are we using your brother's room?"

"He's staying over at Andy's, tonight," Justin whispered. "And my sister's on Brownie Camp this weekend. So we won't get disturbed. It's further away from Mum and Dad's room, too. Mind you don't wake them, when you go up. I'll get the others, and the food. See you there in five."

Liam nodded. He headed for the door.

Liam sat on Lewis's bed. The room had black-painted walls, with posters of old sci-fi and horror movies. He could smell Lewis's laundry bag, which lay in a corner.

He heard Justin creeping, not very softly, up the stairs. Liam smiled. He couldn't see Justin's Mum and Dad leaving their room, even if they did hear a noise. They were keeping well out of it.

Dum-diddy-dum-diddy-dum-dum-dum!

Liam went to the door.

"Give the sacred password."

"Marshmallow."

Liam opened the door. "Pass, friend." He took a look along the landing. "Where are the others?"

"Not coming," Justin said. "Lucas says he's resigned from the Secret Society. And Ben just snored."

He entered the room, closing the door behind him.

"Not really a feast, is it?" Liam said. "With just us two?" He yawned.

"You want to go back to bed?" Justin asked.

"No," Liam said quickly. "You're right. Secret Society. Old tradition. Let's go." He looked blearily at his watch. "It's midnight. Sacred gesture of friendship, please."

Justin raised his hand. "Mates forever?"

Liam copied him. "Mates forever."

He and Justin did a quick street handshake and went: *pvssssshhh!*

"Now, where's the food?" Liam asked.

Justin swung his schoolbag down from his shoulder. He started to open it, sitting beside Liam on the bed.

"What have we got?" Liam peered into the bag. He sniffed. "Euww. Have you still got your PE kit in there? Couldn't you have found something else to bring the stuff in?"

"Ah, stop your moaning." Justin produced a foil-wrapped package. "Here we are. Cocktail sausages. They're from Abbie's birthday party on Wednesday, but they still look OK. Here's some cheese. These are water biscuits, but they seem quite dry. Last yoghurt from the fridge. Cola. Crisps. And… oh." He picked up something from the bottom of the bag. "That's my last sandwich from lunch yesterday." He took a bite from it. "Come on. Tuck in."

Liam wrinkled up his nose.

"What crisps have you got?"

"Cheese and onion." Justin spat out sandwich, and Liam dived for cover. "Or beef and horseradish."

"I don't like horse," Liam said. "I'll have the cheese and onion." He opened the crisps and started to eat. "Ugh, these have gone soggy."

"Have some real cheese," Justin said. "Hide the taste." He unwrapped the sausages and tried one. "I think these get better with age. Come on. Not wimping out, are you? You know the rules. You made the sacred gesture. That means everyone eats the same stuff."

Reluctantly, Liam reached for the sausages and cheese.

"Fun, isn't it?" Justin said. "There's some of Mum's chocolate cake for afters. Sorry there's just the bottle for the cola. I forgot the cups." He took a swig of cola, then offered the bottle. "Want some?"

"Not just yet," Liam said.

Justin stuffed more food into his mouth. "Remember the first one we did, of these? Round at yours, that Bonfire Night? After we made Mrs Hoskins into a guy, with your Gran's old tights?"

Liam grinned. "Yeah."

He burped. He still didn't feel like food. Not at this time of night. The cheese didn't taste right, and the cocktail sausages were already coming back for more.

He'd have to put a stop to these midnight feasts. Now that he and his gang were older, no one except Justin enjoyed them anymore.

Liam had a go at the chocolate cake. He seemed to be eating away at it for ages, yet it never got any smaller. He didn't know exactly when Justin's Mum had made it, but it was like chewing foam rubber.

He suddenly felt very tired again.

"Think I'll go back to sleep, when you're done. Remember, it's Saturday tomorrow... I mean, today. We've got to be at school for the match." He reached down and felt the bed they were sitting on. "Would it be all right to kip here? As Lewis is away? This is a lot comfier than that floor downstairs."

"Yeah, OK," Justin said. Not having a spoon, he was sucking at the yoghurt through a straw. "I'm only along the corridor, if you need anything. I'll wake you up in time for a good breakfast."

They got up, and Justin shook the crumbs off Lewis's duvet.

Liam clambered into the bed.

"Ah, magic." He burped again. "Right. Goodnight."

"Don't let the bedbugs bite," Justin said. He went to the door and switched the light off.

Within seconds, Liam was asleep.

"Liam!" Liam felt himself being shaken. "Liam!"

Liam woke up. He opened his eyes. Justin was standing over him.

He blinked. "What time is it?"

"Morning!" Justin said. He was already dressed in a tracksuit, over his football kit. "Come on! The match starts in half an hour!"

Liam groaned. "So much for you waking me up for breakfast. Aw…"

He struggled out from under Lewis's duvet. He felt terrible. Tired, and achy, and he still had indigestion from the feast.

"Where's Ben, and Lucas?"

"On their way," Justin said. "Come on. We'll take the emergency exit."

He crossed to the door.

"You what?"

Justin led Liam along the landing and to a glass door Liam had never seen before. He opened it.

Liam was met by a blast of cold air in the face.

He found himself standing at the top of a high, metal staircase, like a fire escape.

"This is the quickest way," Justin said. "We don't want to wake Mum and Dad."

He started to walk down the steps.

"Come on."

Liam grasped the metal handrail and followed.

He blinked. "Hey. I never knew you had a garden out here. Thought it was a yard?"

Below them, several large gnomes sat fishing at a goldfish pond. There was a tree with huge red apples, and two bikes stood against an iron fence.

"We could have taken those," Justin said. "But look." He pointed. "The tyres are flat. Someone doesn't like us."

He ran off across the lawn. Liam had difficulty keeping up. That was weird. Normally, Liam was the faster of the two of them by far.

"Come on," Justin said. "I know a shortcut."

Liam followed him along a path of uneven paving stones. There were more trees, but they'd lost all their leaves. There was no one else in sight. Nearby, Liam could see a large, empty warehouse, with a notice that said: DANGER. KEEP OUT.

"Justin…" Liam caught his breath. He went on running. "I don't think this is right."

"Nearly there!" Justin said.

Sure enough, a moment later Liam found himself dashing into the school playground and across to the playing field. Mr Jenkins already stood waiting, in his referee's gear, and both teams were assembled.

"Come on, Liam," said Mr Jenkins. "You're late! Can't have the captain late, can we?"

"Sorry, sir," Liam said. He looked down. He had his football kit on, even though he didn't remember getting changed.

He blinked. Across the playing field, dressed in smart, blue uniforms, stood a brass band. Liam seemed to know one or two of the faces. He turned to Justin.

"I never knew your Dad played the trombone. And what's Cindy from the pound shop doing on tuba?"

"They've come to play us along," said Justin.

Liam would have asked more questions, but Mr Jenkins was already raising his whistle to his lips.

Liam looked again. The whistle had turned into a party blower, like his family had at Christmas. A high-pitched squeak was heard.

The game began.

Ben ran towards Liam, laughing.

"Hey, Liam. What happened to your football kit?"

Liam looked down again.

He was dressed as a circus clown, in a sparkly pierrot costume with big black pom-poms.

The boys of both teams crowded round.

"AAAAHHH!"

"Shut up!" Liam cried.

Above him, in the air, he saw the ball. He heard Jenkins shouting.

"Come on Liam! Catch it!"

"But you can't use your hands…" Liam started.

"CATCH IT!"

Desperately, Liam reached up. The ball was growing… darkening…

It was made of Justin's mother's chocolate cake.

As his hands made contact, the ball exploded, showering him in dry, crumbly chocolate sponge. The hundreds and thousands on the top were running down his neck. The cake was covering his face… enveloping him… he couldn't move his arms, or legs…

"Aaah…" Liam clawed at the cake. "Aaagh! AAGHH! AAAAAAAAAAAGHHHHHHHH!!!!!!!!!!!!!!!!!!!"

"Liam!" Liam felt himself being shaken. "Liam!"

Liam woke up. He opened his eyes. Justin was standing over him.

"What… what happened?"

"You got all tangled up in the duvet!" Justin pulled it aside.

Liam rubbed his eyes. "Must have been dreaming. Hey, that's the last midnight feast I have with you."

"What were you dreaming about?" Justin asked.

Liam avoided Justin's eye. "Never mind. Hey, come on. We'll be late for the match."

"Plenty of time," Justin said. "Mum's cooking breakfast, downstairs. Bacon and eggs. And I think there's some black pudding."

Liam rubbed his stomach. "I think I'll just have toast."

He followed Justin out of the room and along the landing. There was no sign of the emergency exit. He grinned. What a stupid dream.

"Do you want to go through the bathroom first?" Justin opened the door. Liam staggered in. "I had a great night's sleep. Didn't wake up once. And no dreams."

Liam went to the washbasin.

"Lucky you."

He turned on a tap.

A huge hand reached out of the basin and grabbed him by the neck. Liam yelled.

He fought to escape, but the hand held him. He turned.

Behind him, Justin was wearing a top hat, and a long black cape, and a twirly black moustache, and laughing.

"HA HA HA! HA HA HA HA HAAAA!"

"Liam!" Liam felt himself being shaken. "Liam!"

Liam woke up. He opened his eyes. Justin was standing over him.

"No!" Liam dived beneath the duvet again. "Go away!"

"Liam?" Justin frowned. "What's up?"

"Before I come out," Liam's voice said, "I demand you prove you're real!"

"Hey, come on." Justin slid the duvet aside. "You feeling OK? There's been a few bugs, going round school. Not got a temperature, have you?" He made to feel Liam's forehead.

"No!" Liam pulled away. "Prove you're real! When did we first meet?"

Justin looked puzzled.

"First day of school. When you fell in a puddle. I rescued you."

"What are your favourite crisps?" Liam went on.

"Beef and parsnip," Justin said.

"And have you ever had a moustache?" Liam asked. "And have I ever played football dressed as a clown?"

Justin sniggered. "'Course not!"

Liam caught sight of one of the movie posters on the wall.

The Hand From Outer Space.

He sat up in bed. "Mates forever?"

Justin offered his hand. "Mates forever."

They did the handshake, complete with sound effect.

"Now, come on," said Justin. "I want to get at the fried bread before Lucas."

The door closed behind them.

A long, black cape was hanging there.

The Hero

"Has anyone seen my head, please?"

Fletcher and Duane and Parker looked up in some surprise. It wasn't a question often asked at afternoon break.

They were lying on their backs, out on the playing field, soaking up the early summer sunshine. Nearby, footballs whizzed and frisbees flew.

Fletcher opened his eyes to see a tiny girl with brown hair scraped back in plaits from a worried little face. She had small, round glasses and front teeth that stuck out slightly. She looked like a very thoughtful hamster.

She couldn't have been more than five years old. The playing field was Junior territory, and to see one of the Infants there was rare.

Her head was definitely there. He was looking at it. So the reason for the question was unclear.

Then he understood as the little girl held up a small plastic doll. It was very fashionably dressed in a silvery evening gown, but above the shoulders there was nothing there.

"I've been all over the place, looking for it!" the little girl went on. "It was there at lunchtime, then we were outside the classroom, then in the yard..."

"Shouldn't bring toys to school, then, should you?" Duane said. He lay back and closed his eyes. Parker was grinning.

Fletcher sat up straight. "Where were you when you last saw it?"

"At the sand tray," the little girl said. "But I've been digging in there for ages. I found 5p, but no head."

"Why don't you ask the School Buddies?" Parker said. "That's what they're for." He pointed to some older children with green baseball caps and golden badges, who were patrolling the yard. It was a new idea of Mrs Raeburn's. The Buddies were meant to keep things in order and be friends to the younger kids, but the training day had been on a Saturday, and so far only a few people, mainly girls, had fancied the job.

The little girl looked at the ground. Fletcher understood. The School Buddies were big, powerful people, and this little titch was shy.

He stood up, wishing, not for the first time, that he wasn't quite so tall. Someone had once called Fletcher gangly, and he'd put up with years of jokes about giraffes, and being the first to know when it rained.

"Come on. I'll help you look. What's your name?"

"Suzie," the little girl said. She ignored Parker and Duane, and trotted off happily at Fletcher's side.

Fletcher saw a few more grins as they crossed back into the yard. They did make a strange pairing. She was dark, while his hair was fair and spiky. His face was long and hers was round. And then there was the height thing. It was as though Jill had stood in for Jack, and gone to meet the giant.

Fletcher went with Suzie over to the Infants' sand tray, which was standing outside the door that led in to Violet Class.

"You checked this, yeah?"

"Yes," Suzie said.

Fletcher had a rummage nonetheless, getting his fingers sandy. He gave the little water-wheel a quick spin, for old times' sake.

Then he looked at the brightly-coloured plastic shapes. Some of them were for making sand pies, and were hollow…

"Ah. Ah…" He picked up a small red cylinder and poked his finger inside. "Hold your hand out."

Suzie did. Fletcher turned the cylinder upside down, then slapped it like a ketchup bottle.

A small, hairy object fell into Suzie's hand. Her face lit up.

"Let's have 'em, then," said Fletcher. Suzie handed the doll to him, along with the head. "Now, how d'you fix this on? Oh, yeah. Just two clips. There."

He fiddled with the pieces, then with a *snap* they came together. The doll was smiling as he gave it back to Suzie.

"There you go."

He realised that Suzie was smiling, too. She was looking at him in a slightly strange way. They weren't Jill and the giant, anymore. She now looked as Sleeping Beauty might have looked, when she first woke up and saw her Prince.

He could feel himself going red. He was the tallest kid within fifty yards, and felt rather silly, covered in sand and playing with dollies.

From a long way away, he heard Suzie say:

"Thank you…"

She sounded as if she wanted to add "whoever you are", so he quickly muttered:

"My name's Fletcher. Look after… what's she called?"

"Candy," Suzie said. She put the doll carefully into her pocket. Fletcher smiled.

"You'll have to call her Sandy, instead."

He wasn't ready for how much Suzie giggled. Normally, no one laughed at his jokes. He often became one, when Duane was around.

He went quickly back to join his mates. But he could feel Suzie's eyes, still watching him, as he walked over to the field.

He went crimson, as he heard her shout:

"*Thank* you, Fletcher!"

At the end of school, Fletcher had no sooner left the building with Duane and Parker than Suzie came running across the yard towards him. Duane sniggered.

"Hey. It's your girlfriend again."

"Shut up…" Fletcher muttered.

He found himself smiling at Suzie, nonetheless. Fletcher's parents had decided to call it a day after he came along, and he had no siblings. He'd always quite liked the idea of a little sister.

Suzie was holding a large, oddly-shaped iced cookie, in which Fletcher could see a full set of fingerprints.

"We've been baking. I saved this one for you!"

"Oh." Fletcher took it, slowly. "Cheers."

She was waiting, so he took a bite. It tasted OK, anyway.

Suzie stood gazing at him for a moment. Then she turned and ran towards the gate. Two other little girls met her there. Fletcher saw all of them looking over to him, and laughing.

He walked off quickly, before Duane or Parker could speak.

Fletcher went to Swimming Club, then to the mini-mart for his Mum. He decided to take the shortcut home, past the community centre.

This part of the estate really needed work. Some of the council houses looked like they were falling to pieces. The windows needed cleaning, and the corner of one of them was broken. The houses had front gardens, but they were about a quarter of the size of Fletcher's. He suddenly felt quite lucky.

A single, windswept tree hid the end of the street from view. As he passed it, he suddenly saw Suzie, sitting on the kerb. She was tightly holding a pink plastic lunchbox, one of those made to look like a little suitcase, with a handle.

He went over to her.

"Hi."

He was confused to see how her face lit up again.

He looked round, but there was no one behind him. When Fletcher appeared, generally no one noticed.

He had time. He sat on the kerb beside her, getting his school clothes and the shopping bag dirty.

"This where you live?"

"There." Suzie pointed a few houses back up the street. Fletcher saw a slide in the front garden.

"What you doing out here?"

"I've run away from home." Suzie held up the little case. Fletcher looked worried.

"Why?"

"My Mum and Dad were shouting again."

Fletcher looked towards the house. Everywhere seemed very quiet.

"But I haven't gone."

"Why's that, then?" Fletcher asked. "Did you realise you'd miss 'em?"

"No. I'm not allowed to cross the road."

"Oh." Fletcher paused. She looked so fragile. Like a little flower, that might blow away in the wind. "What were you taking?" He tapped the case mischievously.

Suzie brightened. She opened the lunchbox.

"I've got my best scarf. For if I went somewhere nice."

Fletcher saw a pink scarf that looked like silk, but wasn't.

"Oh, that's nice, innit?"

"And my whistle. In case monsters come." She brought out a plastic whistle and blew Fletcher's eardrums out. "And four pound coins I saved up. And my seashell. And my emoji ball. And some string, and four rubber bands. My Mum says you can never have enough rubber bands."

She passed some of the items to Fletcher. He turned them over and over. All her things… all in this one little case.

He kept hold of a rubber band.

"Do you wanna see a trick?"

Suzie looked puzzled. Fletcher placed the band over his first two fingers, stretching it out a little way to show to Suzie. Then he closed his fist. On the palm side, this meant that all four fingers slipped into the band, but he kept this hidden.

"Ready. And… ZAP!"

He opened his hand, and the band seemed to leap straight through to fingers three and four. Suzie's eyes went the same shape as her glasses.

"Do it again!"

Fletcher did it again. And again, and again. He had done the trick nine times before Suzie grew tired of it. Then they sat and talked. There was just her and her Mum and Dad. She would have to go back for her tea, soon. Then her Dad would go out to the pub… Fletcher guessed she felt rather lonely at home.

Eventually, Suzie packed her case again and Fletcher walked her home, as far as the battered iron gate. He watched as she scuttled up the short path to the front door.

He nearly dropped all the shopping as Suzie blew him a kiss.

Fletcher went home and unpacked the shopping for his Mum, before she could see the state of the bag. Then he went up to his room, and looked into the long mirror inside the wardrobe door. He was trying to see what Suzie was seeing.

He was never going to be Prince Charming. He had a horsey face and a grin to match. His ears stuck out, and his nose looked as if someone had spent too long building it and got fed up. The gold stud in his left ear gave him a slightly wicked look…

He closed the wardrobe. Complete mystery.

When he reached into his pocket, the rubber band was still there.

Fletcher woke early the next morning. Usually, his first thought of the day was about breakfast, or football… or being late for school. But today he found himself thinking of Suzie. He wondered what she was doing, right now.

He left the house so early that his Mum stopped to check her watch was right. He was at school twenty-five minutes before the bell. He wanted to speak to Ms Boyd-Williams. She was surprised to see him at this hour, too.

"Yes… of course you can join the Buddy Scheme, Fletcher. We really need more guys from your year." She smiled. "The younger boys don't like girls telling them what to do. But you know you've got to do a training day, and have an interview with Mrs Raeburn?" She picked up a diary from her desk. "The second training day's this Saturday… it takes a few hours, you'd better bring a packed lunch. Then I'll see if I can book you in for interview on Monday. But I'm sure you'll get it. And thank you. We really need someone to work with Purple and Violet Classes."

Fletcher was smiling as he went out into the yard.

He wandered over towards the Infants' zone, and finally caught sight of Suzie. She was on her own and looking lost. Her friends couldn't be here yet.

It was cooler today, and she was wearing a cheap pink coat with a hood. Playfully, he walked up behind her and tipped the hood over her eyes. She looked annoyed, but then beamed as she freed herself and saw who it was.

"*Hi*, Fletcher!"

"I forgot to give you this back." Fletcher found the rubber band. He did the trick once more before handing it to her. He was pleased to see her smile grow wider. "I've just had a talk to Ms Boyd-Williams. I'm going to be a School Buddy. Working with your class."

"Yay!" Suzie did a little leap.

"FLETCH!" Duane bellowed, from the Junior doors. "Are you coming, or what?"

"Gotta go," Fletcher said, rather sadly. Suzie quickly rummaged in her pocket.

"I forgot. Mum and I made these."

She brought out a friendship bracelet, in pink and yellow.

"Aah." Fletcher took it and fingered it. "Cheers, Suzie."

He slipped it onto his wrist, then quickly covered it with the sleeve of his sweater as he went across to Duane and Parker. But Duane seemed to have his mind on other things.

"I saw Austin, before. So there'll be four of us. We can get a lift off Austin's Dad…"

Fletcher blinked. "You what?"

"For bowling. On Saturday."

Fletcher paused.

"Oh. Not sure I can make it."

"What?" Duane looked horrified. "But mate… it's been booked for…"

"I've signed up to do the Buddy Scheme," said Fletcher. "We're training on Saturday."

Duane looked across the yard. "Is this about those kids? Or d'you just want to wear a cap and give orders? You know all the swots do it, don't you? They're just prefects with a fancy name."

Fletcher was silent. Duane led Parker away.

"Come on, mate. We'll find someone who won't let us down. Someone who knows who their mates are."

Fletcher was left standing alone.

Fletcher had quite a few more presents before the end of the week. Suzie brought him a collage she had made… and a slightly squashed toffee bar… and, for some reason, some tadpoles in a jar. Fletcher thanked her for everything, very politely.

He felt guilty when Saturday came, and he found himself going back into school, albeit in his own clothes.

He'd never thought he would choose to be there at the weekend, let alone when Duane and Parker were going bowling.

Mrs Raeburn was there, and Ms Boyd-Williams, and a youth worker from the community centre. There were seven kids training to be Buddies, of various levels of swottiness. Fletcher was the only boy.

They had lessons about dealing with bullying, and about teaching people to play properly. They would be role models for the younger children... they had to be sensible, and patient... it was a big responsibility...

Fletcher listened harder than to any lesson in his life before.

On Monday morning, he went at break-time to Mrs Raeburn's office and had his interview. It was easy, really. She just asked him a few questions about the sort of happenings they'd learnt about at the weekend, and what he would do. Fletcher said sensible and responsible things, and at the end she shook hands with him and gave him his green cap and a golden badge that said SCHOOL BUDDY. As he reached out to take them, the friendship bracelet slid out of his sleeve. He pushed it out of sight.

There was a few minutes of break left, and he went out into the yard with his cap and his badge on. He saw the difference straight away. The Infants were looking at him with a sort of awe. The Juniors seemed to be sliding away from him, looking a bit afraid, as if a policeman had turned up. Duane caught sight of him. Fletcher grinned. Duane turned away.

Fletcher went over towards the sand tray.

"Hey. I'm your new Buddy."

A small crowd of little girls smiled their way over to him.

At their head was Suzie.

"Well done, Fletcher. I'm very proud of you."

Fletcher found himself busier than he had ever been. As well as working with the Infants, he had to do other duties as a School Buddy… making sure kids cleared their trays away after lunch… or taking a turn in the Buddy Corner in the yard. There was a huge plastic lollipop standing beside him that said: FIND A FRIEND HERE. He soon had more friends in the younger years than in his own.

It took up a lot of his time. He had to stay after school to set up games equipment, and be there to help show people around on Open Evening. He wasn't free to laze around or play football with Duane and Parker anymore. But in any case, Duane was still ignoring him. And Parker just did what Duane told him.

Fletcher was happiest when he could just be Buddy to Suzie and her friends. By the end of the first week, he had learned three clapping games and two skipping rhymes. When they played together, he first led them around the corner of the building, so the Juniors couldn't see. But he felt the grins on the back of his neck when he went back into school.

Being a Buddy could be expensive. One hot afternoon, he was leaving school, and found Suzie and five other girls from her class scurrying along behind him. They were all gazing up at him – though it was Suzie who came to hold his hand, and gave the others a warning look. Before he knew where he was, he found himself standing beside a nearby ice-cream van, buying six ice-lollies. That was a whole week's pocket money to Fletcher. The woman in the van gave him a smile.

"Who are you? The Pied Piper?"

Suzie just smiled back.

Fletcher had to wait while they finished their lollies, then he led them back up Station Road to the school. He found four furious Mums and a Nan standing waiting – though Suzie's Mum wasn't there. Suzie held his hand a little more tightly.

"She wasn't feeling very well this morning. Her and Dad were shouting again, last night. Will you take me home?"

Fletcher squeezed her hand.

"'Course I will."

They were a quarter of the way there when they met Suzie's Mum hurrying towards them. It was the first time Fletcher had seen her. She had a pale face and wide, serious eyes, just like Suzie. She was babbling apologies and excuses, and Fletcher had to say: "No worries" quite a few times before she calmed down. She looked stressed out of her mind. Suzie didn't seem bothered. Fletcher supposed she was used to this.

"This is Fletcher, Mum. He's our Buddy. He's been really kind to me."

"Thank you," said Suzie's Mum. She reached out for Suzie. After a pause, Suzie let go of Fletcher's hand. "Come on, love, we need to get your tea over and done with before your Dad gets in."

Fletcher smiled at Suzie, then walked off towards his own house. But he stood watching from the corner, until Suzie and her Mum were out of sight.

"Right," said Duane in the yard on Friday morning. He had decided to notice Fletcher. "No excuses this time. Barbeque. Mine. Tomorrow afternoon. 3 o'clock. With rare breed sausages, and a silent disco. You bring your own music."

Fletcher went quiet. Duane gave him a threatening stare.

"You've not got nothing on this week. I checked. There's nothing happening here tomorrow."

Parker's sharp eyes had spotted a small, yellow envelope sticking out of Fletcher's pocket. He sneaked a hand over and plucked it out. Fletcher made a grab for it, too late.

"Hey!"

Parker handed the envelope to Duane, who took out a small sheet of thin, fancy paper. It was covered with balloons and streamers and teddies.

"*You are invited to Suzie's party! On…*" He looked at the date. "That's tomorrow!"

Parker's eyes grew massive.

"You're going to a *party*? With all them little kids? Haven't you got *no* shame?"

"She'll be six," Fletcher said. "She's not very happy, at home…"

"Fine, then!" Duane tore the invitation into pieces and threw it down. "Go and play with your baby friends! My barbeque's for *grown-ups*, anyway."

Fletcher took a step towards him. For a second, his fist clenched. Duane backed away.

Fletcher saw two other School Buddies watching. He remembered he had his cap and his badge on. He took a deep breath.

He pointed at the remains of the invitation upon the ground.

"Pick that litter up."

He went to join the playground patrol.

Suzie asked Fletcher to arrive early for the party on Saturday afternoon. She said she wanted help setting up. Fletcher remembered the stressed look on her mother's face, and did as he was told.

When he arrived at the house, there was just Suzie and her Mum and an older lady that Suzie called Auntie Barbara. There were two rooms downstairs, a small living room and an even smaller kitchen. Fletcher felt too big for the place.

He had dressed for the occasion. He had his best tracksuit on, and white trainers, and the signet ring he couldn't wear at school and kept for special events. He'd put hair gel on, and aftershave, even though he didn't yet shave. When he opened the wardrobe door to use the mirror, his reflection said to him:

What do you think you're doing?

He was rewarded when Suzie gave him a smile.

"You look very smart."

She was wearing a pink fairy fancy dress costume, with a big red flower in her hair, and looked ridiculously sweet. Fletcher really hoped that no one had seen him coming here.

He told himself, for the fourteenth time, that he wasn't here as a guest, but as a helper. Yes. He was just helping out with the younger kids. He was their Buddy.

There was no sign of Suzie's Dad. Fletcher wondered if he was in the pub again.

He gave her a card, and the new doll in the same series as the headless one. He'd had to break into his secret savings to afford it, and had spent half the morning hanging around a toy shop, pretending to look at tanks and guns, until all the other customers had gone and he could take the doll to the check-out. Suzie looked disappointed for a second.

"I've got this one." She brightened. "That's OK. They can be twins."

She gave him a huge hug.

"Thank you!"

She let him go, and went to pick up a long, thin box from the arm of the sofa.

"Look what Mum gave me."

She opened it to reveal a necklace of multicoloured glass beads on a thin, nylon thread. It looked cheap, but very pretty.

"Will you put it on?"

"I don't think it'd suit me."

Suzie giggled. "No, you silly boy. Put it on *me*."

Fletcher fastened the string of beads around her neck. The clasp was really tricky. Suzie was smiling. So was her Mum, as she entered the room and saw them.

Fletcher helped Mum and Auntie Barbara to set the small table with a party cloth and paper plates and streamers. There were bowls of crisps to set out, and plates of little fairy cakes. He tried not to think about the sausages and burgers at Duane's.

Soon afterwards, Suzie's guests arrived. Fletcher knew many of them from school.

He spent the next hour learning that he never wanted to work in childcare. He couldn't understand how small people could move so fast. They were everywhere, in and out of both rooms, all over the furniture, and Fletcher somehow still felt it was his job to keep them under control. Mum and Auntie Barbara tried to help, with Pass the Parcel and Musical Statues. Fletcher was a statue for so long it made his back ache.

Eventually they all sat around the party table for tea, and the food started to disappear at an incredible rate. Fletcher only had two crisps and a cocktail sausage. He was kept busy passing sandwiches and cakes, and talking.

Just before the birthday cake came in, Fletcher heard Suzie chatting to a little girl with red hair. He had discovered she was Suzie's cousin.

"That's Fletcher. He's my boyfriend."

Fletcher nearly dropped an entire jelly.

The cousin giggled. She looked a year or two older than Suzie.

"Your boyfriend? He's a bit big for you, isn't he? Is he on stilts?"

"He's a very kind person," said Suzie firmly. "And when we get older, we're going to get married."

Fletcher picked his jaw up off the table, and somehow managed to smile as Suzie's Mum brought the cake in, with six candles burning.

They were halfway through the birthday song when Fletcher suddenly looked at the front window and saw Duane. He had his phone, and was snapping one photo of Fletcher after another.

Fletcher met his eye. Duane grinned.

Then he turned and ran.

Fletcher looked at his watch. The barbeque would be starting soon. All the lads were going to be there… and now Duane had something to show them.

Fletcher drank a glass of cold orange squash, very fast.

Suzie blew the candles out in one great gust.

Monday morning at school was one long walk of shame for Fletcher. Everyone seemed to have seen the photos, and he heard the same jokes over and over again.

"How's your girlfriend, Fletch?"

"Did you play Pin the Tail on the Donkey? Oh no, that's *you*, isn't it?"

"When's *your* birthday? You'll be four, won't you? Are you getting a doll's house?"

And so on. Fletcher was starting to hate being a Buddy, and a Prince. He wanted to be an ordinary human being again.

Suzie was looking distinctly stroppy, when Fletcher met her at morning break.

"It's all over the school! Have you been talking about us? What have you been saying?"

Fletcher had the feeling Suzie had been watching the soaps.

"Nothing! It was…"

Suzie took the necklace from her pocket.

"Mend this for me? I can't get it to stay on."

"Probably the clasp again." Fletcher took the necklace and spread it out in his hands. "Look, Suzie…"

The next moment, sixteen beads flew up into his face.

Fletcher gawped as he found himself holding two ends of a nylon thread. There were beads rolling around the yard, bouncing off his shoes… then one fell from the peak of his Buddy's cap.

Suzie was staring at him in horror.

"My necklace… you…"

Some of Suzie's friends had appeared, and were laughing. Fletcher blinked.

"Suzie… I'm…"

Suzie burst into tears and ran into the school.

Fletcher picked up all the beads, and tried to repair the necklace. But it was well and truly broken. He wanted to take the pieces back to Suzie, but the bell had gone, and he had to go into class.

At lunchtime, he managed to get to the door before Violet Class came out into the yard. Suzie was there, with her friends. Fletcher took a step towards her. But she flounced off across the yard, her head in the air. Sleeping Beauty seemed to have lost interest in her Prince.

Fletcher heard a few words floating back.

"Aren't you going to see your boyfriend, Suzie?"

"We've split up. My Mum's right. Men aren't worth it."

Before lunch was over, Fletcher had handed in his cap and his badge. He knew he would never be able to face anyone under seven again. Ms Boyd-Williams didn't say anything. She just gave him that teacher look that says:

You've let the whole school down.

The week went by, and slowly the Juniors started talking to Fletcher. He was able to hang out again with Duane and Parker, though Fletcher knew Duane would never let him forget his time as a Buddy – or the photos.

"Never get involved with girls, mate," he said at break on Friday morning. "You've got to be your own man."

Fletcher nodded slowly. He was quietly playing with the friendship bracelet.

A little boy came running over. He ignored Fletcher, and spoke to Duane.

"Hi. Will you be my friend? I've got one, but he's horrible."

Duane looked up to see a lollipop beside him. Fletcher realised they were standing right in the middle of the Buddy Corner.

"Hey, no… I'm not a…"

Slowly, a smile spread across Fletcher's face.

"Oh come *on*, Duane. You know it's your job to look after people." He looked at the small boy. "Don't worry, he's forgotten his cap. But he'll be your friend. Won't you, mate?"

He put his hands in his pockets and sauntered off towards the playing field. He looked back to see Duane being dragged off by two small hands.

"I want to play hopscotch, but all the girls are in the way. Can you move them for me? And then I need someone to queue for milk and a cookie, 'cause everyone's taller than me. And then…"

The Arms Race

"They're banning *hugging?*" Bethany blinked in horror through her glasses. Beside her, Prisha's mouth opened to the size of a ping-pong ball.

Tessa nodded solemnly. She had the look of a newsreader about to announce another lockdown.

"My Mum heard it at PTA last night. They're worried about bullying. So no one's allowed to even *touch* anybody, anymore. No high-fives, and no holding hands... and no hugs."

"What have they got to do with bullying?" Prisha asked. "Holding hands and hugging's what you do with your friends."

She knew what she was talking about. Tessa and her friends were very close. They often began the day with a big hug, and only a few years earlier they had been known to hold hands on the way home from school.

It was only ten past nine, but already the story was spreading around the school like a stomach bug. Some of the boys had come across the classroom, and were listening.

"They're going to announce it in Assembly this morning," said Tessa. "From now on, everyone has to respect everyone else's personal space. And not invade it."

"How do you invade someone's personal space?" Hamil asked. Next to him, his mate Carlton grinned.

"Like this."

He slid an arm towards Hamil, messed up his hair then got him in a friendly headlock. Hamil laughed and spluttered. He freed himself.

"I can see what they mean," said Prisha. "I mean, that's kind of like bullying."

"Not if you know the guy," said Carlton. He was bigger than he had any right to be, and was one of those boys who like to show off their strength. There was still a chair with a broken back where he had leaned on it.

"You won't be able to mess around like that in future," said Sebastian. His uniform looked very neat, and he was wearing his School Buddy's badge, shining in gold. "We're going to take team points off anyone who breaks the rule."

The other boys took no notice of him.

"Well, I think it's awful about the hugging," said Tessa. "What are you meant to do, when you see your friends? Blow kisses? Write to them? My Mum's really annoyed. But some of the Mums and Dads thought it was a good idea."

"It's only *girls* who hug, anyway," said Carlton.

"It's not! What about footballers? When they score a goal? They all hug."

"Oh, yeah, but that's *man*-hugs. Team hugs."

"They still put their arms round each other, don't they? Great big men, all going…" Tessa did the impression. Everyone laughed, except Sebastian.

"It's going to be difficult," said Bethany. "I like a hug. Makes you feel wanted."

"And what about shaking hands?" said Hamil. "My Dad always tells me that's polite."

"And there's street handshakes." Carlton turned his hand sideways.

"And low-fives, too."

"And then…" Carlton grinned. "There's always…"

He made a grab at Sebastian and started tickling. Sebastian yelped and giggled helplessly.

"Carlton! Get off me!" He pulled away, looking cross as he saw the others laughing. "If you ask me, the sooner they start this ban, the better."

"It's a breach of human rights," said Tessa. "And if *I* was running this school…"

"Well, you're *not*, Tessa," said Ms Boyd-Williams behind her. Everyone jumped. "And the Personal Space Initiative is for the good of all of us. I'll be explaining it properly in Assembly. Now, everyone, back to your places."

The kids scuttled to their seats. But Tessa was looking annoyed. And when Tessa was annoyed, things began to happen.

Ms Boyd-Williams' Friday Assembly seemed to go on forever. There was a story about a horse saving someone's life, during which everyone did their best to keep their faces straight. Then a song called *My World Is Awesome!* Then a show and tell, where you could bring in interesting things, which today featured a piece of volcanic rock, some Roman coins and a kazoo. Bethany sneaked a look at her watch, and risked a mutter to Tessa.

"I'm sure this has stopped. You know some schools don't even have Assemblies, anymore?"

"It's Mrs Raeburn," Tessa whispered back. "She loves this stuff. *And* Ms Boyd-Williams. She's been like this ever since she got made Head of Year. She's gone mad with power."

Bethany pulled a face.

They started to listen a little more closely when Ms Boyd-Williams came to talk about the Summer Fair.

"There'll be the usual games… Tombola… magnetic fish pond… although this year it won't have any water, because of Health and Safety. For the same reason, we won't be having a coconut shy, after what happened to that cat in the garden behind the school last year. But there will be an ethically-sourced barbeque, and a display on Fire Safety."

"Hours of fun for all the family…" muttered Carlton.

"We'll also be having races on the playing field," Ms Boyd-Williams went on. "Though not the dressing-up race, because of the risk of heat exhaustion. And the egg and spoon race will use cotton reels instead of eggs. But there'll be a non-competitive relay race, and the Guardians' Race. That's what we used to call the Fathers' Race, but more inclusive."

"This sounds so boring," Tessa whispered. "They won't get many people at this rate. I'm going to talk to Mum, see if we can liven this up a bit."

"And now…" said Ms Boyd-Williams. "I want to talk to you about an exciting new happening, which will make this school an even happier place to work and play."

It took Tessa and her friends a moment to realise she meant the hugging ban.

"I'm sorry to say that one or two bits of bullying have been going on. And we haven't all been respecting one another as we should. So, as from today, there's to be no touching one another in any way, and everyone has to respect everyone else's personal space. Imagine that everyone has a little bubble of space around them, and you're not allowed to burst it."

Further along the row from Tessa, Carlton did a mime of firing a pop-gun.

"The School Buddies will be making sure everyone keeps to the rule," Ms Boyd-Williams went on. "And anyone found to be upsetting anyone by bursting their bubble will lose points for their team. One point for a small breach of the rule, five points for a serious one. It'll be a good chance for all you Buddies to use your judgment."

Around the hall, School Buddies looked important. Everyone else scowled.

"That's all for now," said Ms Boyd-Williams. "So let's finish off by singing *I'm Gonna Follow My Star*. And then it's time for Maths Games!"

She was beaming. No one else was.

Mr Palmer came forward with his guitar, and the Assembly limped wearily to its end.

Tessa only really started to notice the new rule when morning break arrived. Usually, there were clapping games going on among the Infants, and boys scuffling on the playing field, and one or two hugs, too. Today, there was nothing. The School Buddies were watching, and people seemed afraid even to go near each other. Girls and boys were walking around like robots. Carlton and Hamil and their mates were kicking a ball around as usual, but when TJ scored a goal, Carlton lost a team point for slapping him on the back. When Bethany's little sister fell over and hurt her elbow, Bethany lost a point for kissing it better. Tessa frowned. Most of her friends were on Blue Team with her, and this was going to cost them.

By lunchtime, Tessa had decided to act. She took out her best purple pen. During lunch, everyone saw a piece of paper being slid around, amidst the cheesy fish in batter and mixed fruit cookies.

"I'm organising a petition, against the hugging ban. Would you like to sign… yes, thank you. Oh, and you've put some kisses too, that's great! Now, would you like to sign… no, it's not about the cross-country runs, that was last week. Would you like to…?"

It didn't go as well as she'd hoped. By the end of lunchtime she only had seventeen signatures, and those included Bethany and Prisha and Carlton and Robin

Hood and Get Lost. There were over four hundred students in the school.

"Would you like me to hand that in?" said a voice. Tessa turned in surprise to see Sebastian, in his Buddy's cap. "We've got a School Council meeting, later."

Tessa handed it to him. "Thank you."

Sebastian read it. "You've spelt "privacy" wrong. And "intolerable". Shall I correct them for you?"

Without waiting for an answer, he took out a big, black rollerball pen and scribbled out the two words. Then those on either side. Then the names. He went on scribbling, harder and harder, until the pen actually went through the paper in a huge hole. Tessa made a grab for her petition, and for Sebastian too.

"Stop it! *Stop it!* That's mean!"

Sebastian backed away.

"Watch it. Touch me and I'll have five team points off you, as well. You've got to learn to obey the rules, Tessa. It's for our own good. We don't like bullies, here."

He turned to two younger children, who were wearing plastic gloves and had a black bin bag. They were on litter pick, for breaking some other rule. It was another of the Buddies' powers. Sebastian thrust what was left of the petition into the bag.

"Bin this rubbish."

He walked away from Tessa, head in the air.

Tessa's eyes narrowed…

"It's political correctness gone mad," said Tessa's Mum, on Sunday afternoon. She and Tessa were two of a kind, and had been talking about the hugging ban all weekend. "Didn't we have enough of this during COVID? OK, if a boy or girl's being threatened... but when even friends can't touch each other... It's good for stress, to hug someone or pat them on the back or take their hand. It's been proven."

Tessa's Mum was a Health Visitor and knew these things.

Tessa looked hopefully around the living room. Their audience consisted of her Granddad, in his favourite armchair, who was watching a murder mystery on TV... her Dad, on the sofa, sparked out on Yorkshire pudding and tinned peaches... and her big sister Lois and her enormously tall boyfriend Gavin. None of them looked too worried about human rights.

Tessa tried the teenagers first, as nearest to her in age.

"What about you two? Don't you like to hug?"

For a second, Gavin grinned.

"Yeah, I do."

He slid a friendly arm around Lois, who rolled her eyes. Gavin glanced along the sofa, as Dad woke up. He took his arm back.

Tessa moved along.

"What about you, Granddad? What do you think?"

Granddad looked at the TV.

"I think this film's codswallop. Anyone else watching?"

The teenagers shook their heads.

Granddad took the remote and zapped the channels.

"Any sport on? That's if you don't have to pay extra for every match."

A trailer was coming on, for a sci-fi series. Gavin's face lit up.

"Hey! It's Captain Nine!"

The caption on the screen read: *Captain Nine, Space Explorer*. Then they saw a young woman in a space-age uniform. Granddad pulled a face.

"Used to like this, but they've wrecked it now. Captain Nine's suddenly a woman! More political correctness."

"Granddad!" Lois looked across the room. "That's so sexist!"

"I remember this in the Sixties, when it was cardboard sets and rubber monsters… but the stories were good. Now every show's got to have a woman, and a Martian, and someone purple and a man with three legs…"

Lois buried her face in a cushion.

"I liked it more when it was Mike MacDonald as Captain Nine," Gavin said. "Why can't we have guys as heroes, anymore?"

"I'm with you," said Granddad. "There used to be lady astronauts in cute spacesuits… every week he'd rescue one of them… then fall into an embrace…" He demonstrated.

"Granddad," said Lois. "If you don't stop that I'm going to leave the room."

Mum looked at the actor on the screen.

"Lara Delaney."

"Who?" Dad woke up, again. "What? I haven't got any."

"Lara Delaney. I was at school with her. She went to Sansford High."

Tessa looked round in surprise. Everyone was listening to Mum now.

"Did she?"

"We did Drama GCSE together." Mum laughed. "Turned out to be more use to her!"

"Are you still in touch?" Lois asked.

"No… I think her Mum still lives round here, though. Might have a number, somewhere…"

Tessa forgot the hugging ban, for a moment. She even stopped thinking up ways to torture Sebastian.

"Wouldn't it be great if we could get her to the Summer Fair? We'd really get people in, then. I know lots of kids, love *Captain Nine*. Better than fire safety or races no one can win."

Mum gave her an approving look.

"That's not a bad idea. Mind… it'd probably cost. But I could look into it…"

"Right." Gavin leapt up. His legs seemed to go on unfolding for quite some time. "Are we gonna support Tessa, then? Defy the hugging ban? Come on, peeps. Group hug."

Lois looked at him. She had the face of someone who was thinking of changing boyfriends.

"Come on then, Captain Nine." Granddad stood up. "Only way I'll ever get to hug my grandkids. Lois runs about a mile, every week."

"Excellent idea." Mum came across the room. "Come on, group. De-stress."

Reluctantly, Dad and Lois moved off the sofa. Tessa ran to join in.

They put their arms around each other's shoulders, like a team on the rugby pitch. Tessa hugged Lois, and Granddad hugged Mum, and Gavin was hugging everyone. His arms seemed to fill the room. Tessa heard Lois's voice, then Granddad's.

"This is *so* lame."

"Aah, come on. I can hug my granddaughter, can't I?"

"Dad! That's me!"

"Sorry, son."

"Gavin! Did you put deodorant on this morning?"

Tessa gave a final squeeze. "I love you all!"

They came out of the hug. Tessa and Granddad looked happy. Dad and Lois looked embarrassed. Standing next to Lois, Gavin looked as if he'd been waiting for this all week.

"See!" Mum said. "There's nothing to be ashamed of."

"Right," said Tessa on Monday morning. "My family's given me another idea."

She handed round some flyers she'd made at home. Bethany looked at one.

"The Hugging Club?"

"And we're having our first meeting at lunchtime. Away from the School Buddies. Pass some of these around. We're going to make a space where friends can meet."

Finding a suitable space proved to be difficult. The only place in the school grounds where the Buddies and the lunchtime supervisors never went was the small patch of grass at the front of the building, with its ornamental flowerbed. And that was in full view of the staffroom window, as well as some of the Infant classrooms. Fortunately, it was a hot sunny day and all the blinds were down.

Tessa took a look around. There was Bethany and Prisha and Carlton and Hamil, and two girls from Cedar Class and their little sisters. There was Serena in her wheelchair, and two boys who were even bigger than Carlton and looked as if they were already changing their minds. Everyone was sitting beside the flowerbed, and one of the boys was ruining it by picking at begonias.

Tessa first handed round a tube of Toffos and a large packet of cheese and pineapple whirls. Her flyer had promised *Refreshments*. Once everyone was sucking sweets and munching crisps, they were quiet enough for her to speak.

"Well, hi, everyone. And welcome to the Hugging Club. This is a place where you won't get told off for being with your friends."

"I'm not sure about this hugging stuff," one of the big boys said. "What's it gonna do for our image?"

"You can man-hug too," said Tessa. "Or bear-hug. Or high-five. Anything you like, as long as it's friendly. But let's start with a big group hug. Come on!"

Slowly, awkwardly, they all stood up, while Serena

drove her chair in amongst the group. Most of them now looked as if they were having second thoughts about this. They looked even more embarrassed than Tessa's family.

"Now. We're all friends here. No one's being bullied. So… go for it!"

Arms appeared at all levels as the group hug began. Tessa found herself between Bethany and one of the little sisters, who was nearly half her height. Her back was starting to ache. She could smell the crisps, and the uniform of someone who had already done P.E. But she ploughed on.

"There. Now, isn't that nice?"

From what she was hearing, it didn't sound like it. As with her family, she seemed to have the commentary on.

"Carlton, get off my foot!"

"Euww! You've got chewing gum in your hair!"

"Ow! Serena, that was my ankle! Put your brakes on!"

"This is stupid."

"Garth, stop digging your nails in me!"

They came up for air. Some of the girls looked fairly happy, but everyone else looked red and cross. Tessa took a deep breath. Giving people their rights wasn't always easy.

Carlton nudged her suddenly.

"Hey, hey. Look."

He pointed towards the recycle bin, nearby on the front path. A long nose was watching them from behind it. Tessa knew that nose, and the person who liked poking it into other people's business. She saw the flash as the sun caught a gold badge.

Carlton strolled casually across the grass, then stuck out a hand and gave the nose a pull.

"*Aaarghh!*" Sebastian came out of hiding, very quickly. "Right, that's five points off for your team, Carlton."

"Aah, shut up," said Carlton. "Serves you right for spying."

Sebastian rubbed his nose as he came across towards the group.

"I saw you all! Flouting the ban! Group hugging."

"There's no bullying here," said Tessa. She tried not to look at Carlton. "We're all friends. You could come and join us."

"Sebastian hasn't got any friends," one of the other boys said. "He's a Billy no-mates, aren't you, Seb?"

"Only boy who does group work on his own!"

"Only child! He's so *lonely…*"

"No…" Tessa looked at them. "No… shut up. Shut up! That's not what the Hugging Club's about!"

Sebastian's eyes glittered. Then a smirk came to his face. While the Hugging Club went on bickering, he slipped across towards the staffroom window. It was open. He stood out of sight to one side of it, then reached inside and unfastened the blind.

It came flying up.

Tessa and the Hugging Club turned to see every teacher in the school watching them.

Tessa was not popular for the rest of the day.

"Five team points off! For *all* of us!"

"And it's Monday, so they've taken it off the ones we won last week! You've wiped out my collage, *and* my sponsored judo falls!"

"You can go and find someone else to hug, Tessa!"

At hometime, Tessa still felt angry with Sebastian. Though she was angrier with Carlton and the other boys for provoking him. There really wasn't any excuse for bullying or being nasty. She began to see the point of the ban.

But she refused to be beaten. It wasn't fair that moments of stupid bullying should stop friends holding hands or enjoying a hug.

She walked to the end of the road with Prisha and Bethany, then once they were safely out of sight of the school, she gave each of them a quick hug before heading home. Mum had some leave that week, and was there to greet her.

"I've got *fantastic* news, love! I rang Lara Delaney's Mum. And she remembered me! She didn't want to give out Lara's phone number – I guess you can understand that – but she put me on to her agent. Just had a call back – Lara's agreed to come to the Fair! She'll do it for a donation to her charity, and anything we make on the day can go to school funds. Her agent says we could charge for autographs… or photo opps, maybe…?"

Tessa stopped looking annoyed. She smiled.

"Mum? How about this for an idea…?"

The Summer Fair was causing huge excitement. It was advertised in all the local papers, and online. Everyone was thrilled at the chance to meet the star of *Captain Nine*. A few days before the Fair, Mum had more good news. One of the other actors from the series had agreed to come along.

"You know Jason Burgess... plays Lieutenant Tamar? He does stuff for Lara's charity, too. So there'll be someone for the guys *and* the girls!"

Tessa was pleased. She only watched *Captain Nine* occasionally, but she rather liked Jason Burgess.

She was soon popular again at school, once she let slip that her Mum was Lara's friend, and bringing the actors to the Fair. She even got an approving look from Mrs Raeburn.

She only hoped the teachers didn't discover her plan.

The school had its biggest ever turn-out for the Fair. People came from miles around to see Lara Delaney and Jason Burgess. Tessa's Mum and Dad had set up their big garden tent at the edge of the playing field, and the queue outside was huge. There were people wearing *Captain Nine* badges and t-shirts and even costumes from the series. There were several crewmembers from Space Exploration Service and a couple of hairy monsters in anoraks and trainers.

Tessa was feeling nervous. She hadn't been able to get near the tent yet. She and Prisha were trapped behind their plant stall. Next to them, Sebastian was serving teas and looking superior, with his Buddy's cap and badge on.

What if he found out? What if the teachers found out? Many of them were here, including Ms Boyd-Williams and Mrs Raeburn…

TJ came by the stalls, and helped himself to a cupcake.

"Hey!" Sebastian gave him a glare. "They're 50p! My Mum made them."

TJ grinned. He found some money.

"Aren't you coming to see Lara and Jason? I've just been in there."

Sebastian pouted. He was the only boy Tessa knew who could pout.

"She's not the *real* Captain Nine. It's always been a man, going back to the Sixties. It's not fair. I can't even dress up as him, anymore." He looked towards the tent. "Look, they've even got the title wrong. It's a WORD, not a figure. Any *proper* fan will tell you that."

Tessa saw the sign outside the tent. It said: MEET CAPTAIN 9!

"I quite like it being a woman." TJ ate the cupcake. "And we had a lovely hug."

Tessa could have shoved the cake in his face.

Sebastian's eyes burned.

"*What?*"

"She's selling hugs! Two quid a time. It's all going to school funds…"

Sebastian was going very red. He was already

marching off towards the tent, straightening his cap as he went. Tessa ran after him.

"Sebastian… it's all right… it's for charity! They're both DBSd…"

Sebastian pushed his way past the queue.

"Excuse me! School Buddy. Official business."

Tessa entered the tent a moment or two behind him. She felt her heart skip as she saw two of the stars of *Captain Nine*, right in front of her. Jason Burgess was sitting behind a picnic table which was covered with promo photos and postcards. He was signing some for a girl and a boy from Pine Class. Lara Delaney was giving a big hug to a tall, bald Dad who looked as if his world was now complete. She was smiling. Nearby, another sign gave the prices for autographs and photos – and hugs.

"It's quite cool, this. Good way to keep the fans happy. It's nice to see everyone together. All this rubbish about me being a woman, and why it's bad I'm a woman, and why it's good I'm a woman… I thought I was cast because I was the best person to play the part."

"Hey!" Sebastian glared at her, and at the Dad. "You can't do that! This is a no-hugs school!"

There was laughter, and some jeering from the children. Some of the parents looked shocked at Sebastian's rudeness.

Sebastian turned on Tessa.

"*You* did this! You and your meddling Mum. You knew…"

Tessa gave a peacemaking smile, but Sebastian shoved past her and out of the tent.

"Right! I'm going to get Mrs Raeburn."

Tessa stopped smiling.

Her Mum came over. She wasn't looking as sure about the idea as she had at home.

"Oh dear. I hope there's not going to be trouble about this."

She turned towards Lara.

"Thanks so much for doing this, the kids are loving it – you seem to have got a lot of grown-up fans, as well…"

"I love them," said Lara. "Comes with the job. Without them, we wouldn't have a show. No one to explore space with us."

The tent-flap parted, and in came Ms Boyd-Williams and Mrs Raeburn. Tessa suddenly wanted to sink through the grass and disappear. Sebastian stood behind them, with a face that said: *so there!*

Mrs Raeburn gave Lara and Jason her most professional smile.

"Hi! Thank you for coming, it's made such a difference to our Fair." She held out a hand. "Letitia Raeburn, I'm the Head here… this is Kay Boyd-Williams, Head of Year…"

The tent was full of children exchanging glances and mouthing: *Letitia?!*

Jason came to join in the handshakes.

"Hi. I'm Jason."

Mrs Raeburn looked at him and smiled. As she shook hands, she seemed as excited as the children.

"Hi, lovely to meet you." She reached into her jacket pocket. "Well, I think it's time I gave something to school funds, too. Are you...?" She paused. "Are *you* doing the hugs, as well?"

Jason smiled. He really did have a lovely smile. Tessa had often noticed it, on TV.

"Yeah. Sure."

"But..." Sebastian's eyes bulged.

Ms Boyd-Williams looked doubtful for a moment. "Mrs Raeburn..."

Mrs Raeburn looked back at her. She lowered her voice.

"That reminds me, Kay, we need to have a word on Monday about this Personal Space Initiative. I think it might be more trouble than it's worth."

She dropped two pounds into Tessa's Mum's ice cream tub, stepped forward and had an enormous hug from Jason. There were cheers and people going: *ooh!* Tessa's Dad stepped forward with his camera, and quickly took a photo.

"That'll be another two quid."

Tessa looked at Mrs Raeburn in surprise. Somehow, you never thought of your Head doing human things like watching TV.

Mrs Raeburn's hug seemed to have set off a chain reaction. Lara was now hugging another fan dressed as an Interplanetary Commissioner, and Jason was getting ready to hug Ms Boyd-Williams, and Mum was hugging Dad... Lois was here too, and was disappearing into a hug from Gavin.

Tessa went over as Prisha and Bethany entered the tent, and hugged them. Everyone now knew that the ban was over.

Only Sebastian was left on his own. Tessa went to him.

"Never mind, Sebastian. No hard feelings, eh?"

She flung her arms around him and gave him the biggest cuddle of the lot. Sometimes, people just needed a hug.

Sebastian didn't seem to be enjoying it. He spluttered and yelled.

"Stop it! Help! Miss! Mum! *Anyone!* She's invading my personal space…"

Onward and Upward

"Right," said Mrs Hoskins at registration. "Natalie, put that phone away. Jordon, put that boy's head down. Now. As those of you who were listening will know, today is Transition Day. That means everyone gets to visit their new class, and their new teacher."

A buzz of excitement ran around Holly Class. Mrs Hoskins' pupils had the look of a group of prisoners about to get out of jail. It had been a long year. Mrs Hoskins scowled.

"The feeling's mutual. Now, this morning Pine Class will be coming up to us, with Mr Palmer. They'll be with us until lunchtime, so I want you to give them a good welcome, and be mature, helpful and kind. Ha ha. I'll give you some time to talk to them, show them around and see what we do in a senior class. I'll need a couple of people to tell them about team points, the money rota and how the classroom works."

Several hands went up. Mrs Hoskins ignored them.

"Tariq… and Eliza. The rest of you, do all you can to make them feel they belong here. Now, I've read about Transition Days where they have burgers, and games, and art and I.T."

Another buzz ran around the room.

"But we won't have any of that bilge here. I've got a nice quiet worksheet, about rules and being responsible, and you can do it together. Then this afternoon, *you'll* be visiting *your* new classroom."

She smiled for a moment.

"There's a little surprise waiting for you."

"Wonder what the surprise is?" said Zacky, when registration was over.

"Maybe she's retiring," said Dean. "She looks old enough."

"I can't wait for next year," said Natalie, over the back of her chair. "Mr Palmer's cool. He wears a purple jacket. And he does mind reading in Maths lessons."

"There's so much to tell them about," said Tariq, who was looking slightly stressed. "I've spent a year getting this classroom right. How can I pass it on, in a morning? They'll never understand my stationery table. Ow!" He removed a small piece of paper from his ear.

Jordon lowered his hand.

"Can't wait to see the back of *her*." He jerked a thumb towards their teacher. "Palmer's gonna be a pushover. They say he never punishes you. Just makes you write an essay on the error of your ways. I'll have a template ready. Put the details in, and print it off."

"Wish *you* were moving," said Eliza, from next to Natalie. "Might get some peace."

Jordon made a truly terrible face at her.

Zacky looked towards the door.

"Here they come."

Pine Class was entering, accompanied by Mr Palmer. He wasn't wearing purple today, but was in a blue jacket and a yellow tie. He was young and still enjoyed teaching.

The pupils of his class looked small and nervous. Zacky blinked.

"Whoa. Were we ever that tiny?"

"No," said Jordon. "The younger kids have shrunk. Must be all that rain."

"Remember what Mrs Hoskins said," Eliza put in. "We need to make them feel at home. Show them how everything works."

"Yeah," said Jordon. He was grinning. So was Zacky. "'Course we will."

Eliza turned back to her own table, to Natalie and her friends Susie and Abigail.

They were grinning too.

"This is the stationery table," said Tariq. "White paper here, colourful paper over there. Now, it's absolutely vital that you put the felt pens away with all the tops on. Otherwise, people get pink and orange hands when they pick them out. I'll be coming back in here for English, so please make sure you get it right."

"Now that you're in a big class," said Eliza beside the team board, "you have to go round and collect all the team points on a Friday, and give them in to Mrs Raeburn. Then, after lunch, you go round with any change that people have dropped, and say: "Has anyone lost any money?" Don't say: "Has anyone lost a pound?" because some lying low-life will nick it."

"Mrs Hoskins is the teacher from your worst nightmares," said Jordon. "You've just signed your lives away for a year. You know Frankenstein's Monster? Mrs Hoskins taught him Maths."

Sitting opposite him, Arthur and Herbert were looking anxious. Zacky took up the tale.

"You can't talk, can't breathe, nothing. She gives out detentions like sweets. Except there are no sweets. You ever seen that skeleton, in the medical room? They say it's someone she caught chewing in class."

He looked round to make sure Mrs Hoskins wasn't nearby. He was safe. She seemed to have left the room. Mr Palmer was just far enough away, talking to some of the other kids about the school football team.

"'Course," said Jordon, "there *are* ways to make her happy. When she comes in, of a morning, she likes everyone to stand up, don't she, Zack?"

"Does she?" Zacky said. Beneath the table, Jordon kicked him. "Oh! Yeah! That's right. Stand up."

"And then," said Jordon, "she likes to see you're ready to work. So get your pencils out, and chuck 'em on the table. She'll like that."

At the next table, a similar talk was going on.

"You'll be doing French next year," said Susie. "Mrs Hoskins is, like, *really* into France. Brings a baguette and Brie for lunch, every day. And she likes us all to practise our French, whenever we can."

She was struggling not to smile. She knew full well

that Mrs Hoskins had spent the whole of the school trip to France looking for a fish and chip shop. She had voted to leave the EU and would have liked to move Britain further away, as well. She spoke French like a hyena with a sore throat.

"So, when she comes in, in the morning, everyone gets up and says: *Bonjour, madame!* Pass it on."

Worriedly, Hazel and her friend Jessie did. Within a couple of minutes, all the girls of Pine Class had been told to greet their teacher in French.

"Then there's hair," said Abigail. "She hates you to have your hair pinned up, or tied back. You've got to let it down."

"But mine's really long..." said Hazel. She met Abigail's eye. "OK."

She let her hair loose. It started heading for the floor. Abigail blinked. Hazel could have stood in for Rapunzel.

"Make sure there are marker pens for the board, every morning," said Natalie. She handed over two pens from Tariq's table. "A red one and a blue one. Like these."

"But those are..." Susie started. Then she looked at Natalie. She fell silent.

"Go and put them on the board now," said Natalie. "So they're there when she comes back. Show her how helpful you are."

Jessie, Hazel and Hazel's hair zoomed off across the room. There was a big, fat smirk on Natalie's face, and Susie and Abigail were giggling.

Everyone scooted into their places as Mrs Hoskins

re-entered. They saw her have a brief word with Mr Palmer, and pass a key to him. Then he left the room.

"Right!" bellowed Mrs Hoskins. She stepped before the two classes. "Now…"

Her mouth fell open as all the girls and several of the boys of Pine Class leapt to their feet. Arthur, Herbert and their friends threw their pencils onto the table with a deafening clatter. The girls' hair was flying as all of them said:

"*Bonjour, madame!*"

"ARE YOU OFF YOUR ONIONS?" bawled Mrs Hoskins. "SIT DOWN!"

Pine Class had never sat down so quickly in their lives. Jordon and Natalie and their friends were stuffing their fists into their mouths. Only Tariq and Eliza looked embarrassed. Pine Class was catching on. Eyes and mouths narrowed, from table to table.

"Now…" said Mrs Hoskins very menacingly. "We're going to do some worksheets, to find out more about one another. And they're all about *you*, your *family*, your *hobbies*, and what you…"

She was writing all these words on the whiteboard. Then she looked at the blue pen she was using. She rubbed the words with her hand. They stayed put.

"All right, what clown put permanent markers on…?"

She had a ferocious glare on her face, but wasn't sure where to aim it. There were a great many jokers in Holly Class, and they had spent a year learning to keep their faces straight.

She broke off as Mr Palmer returned to the room. With him was Mrs Raeburn. She spoke to Mrs Hoskins, then turned to face the crowded classroom. Everyone started to behave.

"OK, everyone. I'm glad to see you getting to know one another so well. And Pine Class – welcome to your new home. Now, it's time for the surprise announcement... shall I, Mrs Hoskins...?"

Mrs Hoskins grunted.

"Very soon, you'll be moving classes. And classrooms. But you won't be moving teachers. You see, Pine Class, we've got somebody new coming in September to teach the year you're in now. And so, Mr Palmer will be staying with you, and Holly Class will be staying with Mrs Hoskins. Same class names, new year group..."

A sort of muffled howl ran around the room. Suddenly, Pine Class was smiling. Jordon's jaw was heading for the table, and Natalie's face had *Noooooooooooo!* written all over it. Only Eliza and Tariq seemed not to mind.

"So we'll be together for another year," said Mrs Hoskins, with a sort of grim satisfaction. "And I shall expect to see a *much* higher standard of behaviour, now that you're a year older. Now, worksheets. About you, your family, and..."

Jordon looked round, as a piece of paper hit him in the ear.

It came from Arthur's hand.

Last Day

Above the junior entrance hung a huge banner.

FAREWELL YEAR 6 – AND GOOD LUCK!

The bell rang.

Instantly, the doors flew open, and several junior classes piled out. The Year Sixes were the fastest of all.

From the back of the crowd, Liam and Justin emerged. Close to them were various other members of Juniper Class, who were Juniper Class no longer. They had reached the top of the tree.

Liam was grinning.

"Holidays! And freedom. No more kids' school for us, mate. Six weeks off! And then we're off to school with the big guys."

Justin had his hands in his pockets. Unusually for him, he wasn't fidgeting or fiddling. He was looking thoughtful.

"Big school's gonna be cool. They've got brilliant stuff for sport there – great big playing fields, and a basketball court. Not like that little bit of grass we play on. We'll be the stars of Sansford High."

A group of girls came up to them, led as always by Kimberley.

"Bye, Liam!"

"Bye, Kimberley."

"Horrible knowing you."

"Rotten knowing you, too."

"Hope your holiday stinks."

"Yeah. Drop dead."

Kimberley came forward. Then suddenly, she flung her arms around Liam's neck and gave him a big smacker on the cheek. The other girls were laughing. Liam squirmed and wriggled.

Justin bit his lip, as Kimberley stepped away. Liam seemed to be in shock.

Kimberley and her crowd went off laughing towards summer.

"*Euwww!*" Liam frantically wiped his face with his sleeve. "I think I've got rabies." He took a deep breath. "Glad they're not going to Sansford High. Always wondered why this town had a school just for girls. Now I know. It's to keep the rest of us safe."

"Liam," said Justin slowly. "I've got something to tell you."

Ben and Lucas and Daniel came by. Liam turned to them.

"Guys, don't forget. My place, later. End-of-school party. Pizza, ice cream, NetBox. We're not going to bed 'til three."

Ben met Justin's eye. Quickly, Justin shook his head.

"No, OK, Liam. See you later. I'll just let you and J... er... yeah."

He marched off towards the gate, taking the others with him.

"What's he on about?" Liam asked. *"I'll just let you and J… er… yeah*? What's that supposed to mean?"

Justin opened his mouth, then closed it again.

Liam swung his schoolbag onto his shoulders.

"Come on. I've been planning this. Tour of the yard. One last time. Last look at all our memories, before we move on."

Slowly, Justin followed.

No one else wanted to stay in the yard, and they were on their own as they walked across towards the field. Liam was growing quieter. It was some time before he spoke.

"Good times, weren't they?"

"Yeah," Justin said.

"Just think, J. All the times we've lined up out here. All the times we played football on that field. Poor old Jenkins. He'll never get another team like us."

"And we played in the yard, too," Justin said. "How many times did we land our football on the roof?"

"You did, you mean. And you landed me in hospital, when the football went on our shed. And gave me all your colds, and chicken pox."

"Saved your life on the first day, though, didn't I? When we were little. Fished you out of that puddle."

"Yeah, and dropped my satchel back in."

"Well, I only had little hands, then."

"That's true. You've got *really* good at messing things up for me now. Dunno what you'll be like when we're sixteen, like your Lewis."

Justin fell silent again.

They turned back towards the school. They walked past the hall windows. The huge space looked so empty.

"Shame we never did our panto," Justin said. "I thought that was good, your script. No, I really did, mate. No messing."

"Talent show went well, though," Liam said. "'Specially your impressions. And the magic tricks. Hey, hey. Do that coin trick for me."

"Now?"

"Yeah, now."

Justin reached into his pocket for a pound coin. He held it out to Liam on the palm of his hand, then flicked his fingers. The coin disappeared.

He removed the coin from the back of Liam's head. Liam laughed.

"Nice one."

They walked back into the centre of the yard.

"We'll have to go, soon," Justin said. "Everyone's gone. Don't want to get locked in."

"Weird to think there'll be another Juniper Class, next year. I mean, that's like, us. There'll be other people in our classroom…"

Justin took a deep breath. "Liam, listen. I've got to tell you something."

"Never mind. New horizons. New school. New class."

"I'm not coming to Sansford High."

"Then we'll make new mates. Whole new team. By the time we leave school, I'll be ready to be a football star."

"I'm moving."

"Someone told me new kids get bullied there, but not me. Just let 'em try. They'll find out you don't mess with Liam."

"We're going to live in Luton."

"I've got so many plans for *what*?" Liam stood staring at his friend. "What'd you say?"

"We're moving." Justin took a step back, uneasily. "We're going to Luton. My Dad's got a new job there. He says he's sick of delivering the mail... it's not the job he trained for... there's a job going there in a car factory. Loads more money. And Lewis is going for an apprenticeship there. So I'm going to school there and Abbie's going to another school there and Mum's already packing and we're leaving in, like, three weeks, and I did try and tell you, mate, but you never ever listen!"

He paused for breath. Liam still wasn't moving.

They stood in the empty yard for what felt like another term. The school seemed to be on pause around them.

Finally, Liam said:

"Now I know what Ben meant. Does he know?"

Justin nodded.

"Do the others know? Have you told Danny boy? And Lucas?"

"And the girls."

"And the...! And I guess Jenkins knows. And Mrs Raeburn? And right... yeah... I'm only your best mate... *so everyone flaming knows, except me!*" Liam turned and kicked a cola can halfway across the yard.

"Liam." Justin blinked. "Don't swear."

"Why didn't you tell me? How long have you known?"

"About a month. I've been trying to tell you, all that time."

"And what? You can't talk to me?"

"Not totally, no. You only ever want to hear what you want to hear."

"What?"

"I was frightened."

Liam laughed, a short, sharp laugh. "Frightened? Of me?"

"I don't like it, when you get angry. You start taking it out on people. Like me."

"Excuse me? Is this the same Justin who was getting bullied in Infants, 'til I came along? The little fat Justin who…"

"I'M NOT FAT!"

"I took you away from that. Turned you into my second-in-command, and…"

"Oh, don't be so stupid! We're not little kids, anymore! You try talking like that at big school."

"Ooh! The rabbit's grown teeth, has he?"

"Rabbits have got teeth! You call me thick?"

A window of the school opened. Mrs Raeburn looked out.

For a moment, Liam and Justin stared at her.

Then, as one, they turned to leave the yard.

They walked down the path together for the last time. The gate was still open, but the Site Manager would be coming soon to lock it.

They stepped into the street outside.

"So much for farewell tours," Justin said. "And Mrs Raeburn. She's sure gonna remember us."

Liam laughed, for a moment. He looked back at the school, then at Justin.

"Look, mate…"

"I should have been stronger," Justin said. "Should have told you. I didn't want you to find out this way. I'm sorry."

Liam paused.

"Was I really that bad? Were you actually scared of…?"

"No, no!" Justin went and put an arm around Liam, who automatically pushed it away. "Look, you've been a fantastic mate, mate. We'll keep in touch… you could come and visit…"

"Luton's miles and miles away!"

"It's got a carnival."

"I don't care if it's got Durwyn the Dragon's Animation Adventure! What am I meant to do, without you?" Liam stopped. "What I'm trying to say is… you've been my Number Two since Day One, and… like… everything… and you did all the stuff I did… and… ate the food I didn't want… and… messed things up for me, always, but… you were there, too… and you're my mate and I don't want you to go, you big twit."

Justin looked down to see Liam digging his nails into the palms of his hands. He was holding his breath now, too. Justin knew Liam, and knew why.

"You've still got Ben, you know. And Danny boy,

and Lucas. They'll be with you. And we've got the Internet. We can have face time..."

"With a face like yours, why bother? OW!" Liam grabbed his side in pain.

Justin took a final glance at the sign by the gate.

Station Road Primary School.

"Guess we've got to go now. It's been fun."

"Yeah." Liam swallowed. "Yeah, it has."

He moved nearer to Justin.

"You're still coming to my farewell party, aren't you?"

Justin walked off towards Liam's house.

"You try and stop me."

"And we'll eat pizza, and ice cream?"

"'Til we puke."

"And we'll play football in the garden, like we used to?"

"Five-a-side."

"Four-and-a-half-a-side, in your case."

"And you're coming to Luton, whether you want to or not. I'm the one giving the orders now, mate."

"Yes, sir."

"Mates forever?"

"Yeah. Yeah, mates forever."

Behind them, the Site Manager clanged the gate shut.

In the yard beyond, there was a *thud.*

A football had rolled off the roof.

The Real David Ashwood

"And now, just one more. Standing by the stairs… yes, that's it. Smile! Smooth your hair back… OK. Take your hands out your pockets! Now, make sure we can see the badge…"

"Nan!" Paul moved away from his grandmother's ancient camera, and towards the door. "I've got to go!"

Nan lowered the camera. She looked at him proudly.

"I can't believe it. My little grandson, off to big school. Your Mum and Dad would be proud of you." She made a last attack on Paul's blazer with the clothes brush. "Off you go, then. You got your key, 'case I'm not back first…"

"Yeah, Nan!"

"And you know which bus stop…"

"It's *one stop*, Nan! I couldn't get it wrong if I tried!"

"One last thing." Nan smothered him in a big hug, topping it off with a kiss. Paul squirmed. "Have a good day. Remember – there's nothing to be afraid of."

Paul gave her a final smile, took up his schoolbag and left.

He walked up the path and along the street with massive confidence. He'd never worn a blazer to school before. It made him feel smart and grown-up.

It was only when he turned right at the end of the street, instead of left, that he started to feel a little nervous. Left was the route to his old primary school. Suddenly, Paul felt he would have quite liked to go that way. The route to the right led to a crowded bus-stop, filled with people he didn't know.

He was being silly. He'd just said it to Nan – it was only one stop! He had to be a big grown-up lad, for her. She had dreamed of this day. The Masterville High School for Boys was a good one. It had been their first choice.

School for Boys. That would be a bit strange. Paul had never been a big fan of girls, but he was used to them being around, in the classroom. All these other blazers were filled with boys...

He got on the bus. And, even before it had moved off, he was starting to feel worse. He knew this feeling. He thought it had gone. He had to stop it. He had to be the one in charge. Conquer his fears. His therapist had said as much.

"There's nothing to fear, Paul, but fear itself. You need to stand up to it. You need to tell yourself: *I can do this.*"

Paul looked around the bus, in the hope of finding a friend. All his old mates had gone to different schools. He would have to start again. Meet new friends. Masterville was a much bigger school than his old one. And he didn't even know who his form teacher was. They'd been told it would be someone new.

He took a deep breath. He had to squash the fear. He had to do this, for Nan, and for Mum and Dad.

There were one or two younger kids here. They must be Year Five or Six, going to the Masterville First School next door. Paul noticed that their uniform was just the same as his, except for the blazer on top. They had the same grey jumpers and trousers and the black tie with thin silver stripes.

They were talking, and laughing, and scuffling, and doing all those primary school things. Paul really wanted to be with them. They were at the top of the ladder, at their school. Not at the bottom, like him. They were the ones who really had nothing to fear. And there were girls at the First School.

He saw that one of the younger boys was sitting across the aisle from him, separate from the rest. His tie was halfway out of his jumper, he had silver stud earrings and a face that was made to give cheek. He might as well have been wearing a sweater with REBEL written across it.

He gave Paul a grin.

"You look nervous. Your first day in the Slammer, is it?" He sniggered as he saw Paul's face. "That's what they call the big school. So they tell me."

"Are you new here too, then?"

"Yeah. We moved here. I'm meant to be going into Year Six."

Lucky him.

"But I'm not going."

Eh?

"Why not?"

"I don't want to. No one tells me what to do. They

can make me get on a bus, they can make me go to school, but they can't make me stay there. It's a nice day. Got it all planned out. I'm off down the park this morning. Kebab for me lunch, then playing snooker in me mate's uncle's pub. He won't care I'm not at school." He gave Paul a sly look. "You want to come?"

Paul shook his head.

"Thought not. You're a good boy, aren't you?"

The bus was coming to a halt.

"Well, if you change your mind. Me name's David. I'll be at the Flying Fox, 'bout two. We can watch TV in the back room, after. Bye for now."

He was off the bus and gone before Paul could look round.

Paul glanced out of the window. No sign of him…

What a boy. Paul knew Nan wouldn't have liked him.

He stared at the two Masterville buildings. They were right next to each other, the secondary and the primary schools, with their yards adjoining at the rear. Kids in blazers were going into one, kids without were going into the other. Parents in cars were dropping more of the younger ones.

That boy, David. How stupid was he? A lovely primary school to go into, and he couldn't be bothered. They would catch him. They always caught kids who bunked off…

"Oi." The bus-driver's voice cut in. "Are you going?"

Still with the nerves churning inside him, Paul got off the bus.

Afterwards, Paul couldn't remember the walk into school. He seemed to move instantly from one place to another, like in a nightmare. The next thing he knew, he was in a maze of corridors, trying to find his way. The other kids seemed to have disappeared, and he was on his own. He must have taken a wrong turning.

He knew the day started in his form room. Number 37. So why couldn't he find it? All these corridors seemed to have moved, since Induction Day. He took the stairs to where he thought it was. And it wasn't. Where was he meant to be?

He wandered around the first floor. His heart was thumping, and his breakfast was going round inside him like laundry in a tumble dryer. He was trying to remember what the therapist had said, but her voice was far away now. He couldn't hear it. He hadn't felt like this since… since that night. He mustn't remember that night. He had buried it, along with his fear.

Finally he found the right corridor. There was still no one else in sight. He looked at his watch. He was eleven minutes late now. On his first morning. Already, he had let Nan down.

He was longing to be back at primary school. You knew your way, there. You were in the same room all day. All your mates were around you. You were safe.

Here was the room. Here was the door. 37.

He didn't want to open it. On the other side was a teacher, who would tell him off for being late. And a form he'd never met before, who would grin and smirk at him. He wasn't going in there. He couldn't…

He tried to hear the therapist's words. He reached for the door-handle.

And then he heard the bellow. It was a man's voice, and it seemed to make the whole school shake.

"*I* AM IN CHARGE OF THIS FORM! AND I WILL NOT TOLERATE DISOBEDIENCE! I AM IN CHARGE! *AND-YOU-ARE-NOT!!!!!!!!!!!*"

Paul's hand fell to his side. He turned back from the door, leaned against the wall. He was gasping. He couldn't get his breath. The therapist's voice had gone now. The only person he could hear was Nan, on that night.

Paul. Sit down. I've got something to tell you, love. It's… it's your Mum and Dad…

Paul ran. He didn't know where he was going. He only knew that nothing could make him open that door, and face the owner of that voice.

In thirty seconds, he was down the stairs and out of a rear door into the yard. He flattened himself against a wall. Everyone would be in classrooms by now. No one must see him from the windows. He wasn't a boy at school anymore. He was a soldier on the battlefield, running for cover.

He wished he had gone with David now.

How could he escape? He was on the wrong side of the school.

He slid along the building, and then around other, smaller buildings, doing his best to make his way across the yard.

Then he saw the open gate. It was in the fence that separated the two schools, and some careless person had left it unfastened. There were trees, around the fence. If he could get through that gate, he would be out of sight of anyone in this terrifying school.

Paul took a deep breath, and made a dash for it.

He expected at any moment someone to shout his name, challenge him, appear in front of him to bar his way. But there was no one. He had both yards to himself.

He was in the primary school playground now. It was easy to tell the difference. This yard had multicoloured lines painted across it, and cute little benches everywhere, and a climbing frame and slide for the Infants.

Where to now? He was in just as much danger here. There were classroom windows at all angles. Someone must see him…

Again, he dived into the shadow of the building, slid his way around. There was a path to the front of the school, but he could see a locked metal gate at the end of it. There was only one chance. He would have to go through the school, and somehow slip out of the front entrance. He didn't know how many teachers and kids he would have to pass, but this was the only way.

He grabbed the handle of an exterior door. That was open, anyway. He ducked inside, and found himself in a cloakroom of the old style, with wooden benches and low pegs and a door to the toilets.

He sank onto a bench, among other kids' coats. He had to breathe…

He was far, far too hot. He pulled the school blazer off, chucked it across the bench. Beside it he dropped the schoolbag he was still holding. He was roasting inside his jumper.

He couldn't stop here long. Someone would find him. He had to complete his escape…

"Hi."

Paul's heart leapt. A boy in the First School uniform had come out of the loo and was standing beside the bench. He was dark-haired and dark-skinned and had a round, smiley face. He didn't look much younger than Paul.

"Are you the new guy? Miss is waiting for you."

Paul couldn't speak. He goggled at the boy.

He realised that their uniforms matched. The blazer had slid down behind the bench. The boy couldn't have seen it.

Paul was relieved to see a friendly grin.

"Come on. We're down here."

In a dream, Paul followed him out of the cloakroom, past display boards and a fish tank and a library area, and into a large, open plan classroom.

He saw boys and girls who looked more or less his own age, all in their grey jumpers and trousers or skirts. He saw the teacher. She was quite young, a light-skinned woman in a brightly-coloured skirt, a smart jacket and a pink hijab which framed a face that was very beautiful. It looked as if it had been wrapped up because of how special it was.

As Paul entered she pointed at him, slightly mischievously.

"David?"

"He was in the cloakroom, miss," said the other boy. The teacher nodded.

"Thank you, Salim. You're quite late, David. Over twenty minutes."

Paul swallowed. He knew he had to say something.

Nan had brought him up always to tell the truth.

"Sorry, miss. I got lost. I went across the playground, and through a door…"

Some of the class tittered. The teacher smiled.

"All right. I'll believe you, this time." She beckoned Paul to stand beside her. "I'm Miss Amari. Year Six – this is David Ashwood. David's just moved to this town. Now, I want you all to be very welcoming to him, and show him everything we do. David – there's a place for you over here."

Paul fell into a chair. Salim was on one side of him, and on the other was a long, lanky boy with about a million freckles, and flaming red hair. Paul had met plenty of ginger-haired people, but this guy looked as if his head was on fire. He gave Paul a grin.

"Right, then!" said Miss Amari. "New year – new term – and new lessons. Someone help me pass these worksheets round. Time I learnt about my new class. You can all write a bit about yourselves. Then we'll get the board going, and you can watch the English Programme."

It was as if all Paul's dreams had come true. He had gone back in time. He was back at primary school, in a friendly classroom, with a nice teacher, and high school was still a year away.

There was nothing else to do but join in with the lesson. Most of his stuff was in his blazer or his schoolbag, but he had a pen. He did the worksheet, remembering at the last moment to write David instead of Paul. What was the surname? Ashwood. He didn't know much about David, so he just wrote about himself, and his own hobbies, and his own likes and dislikes. He wrote neatly. This teacher was kind, and he wanted to please her.

They watched the English Programme, then did some Maths games. They were all topics Paul had done a year ago, so it was easy for him. He put his hand up a couple of times, answered questions, and got smiles from Miss Amari.

Paul had never felt so lucky. Everyone else was suffering next door, and he had a whole bonus year of primary school still to go. Lunch at the First School was good. He had an all-day breakfast with scrambled eggs, bacon, hash brown and beans, followed by ginger sponge and custard, then went out into the yard and kicked a ball around with the other boys. They were all being very welcoming to him. There was Salim, and a chubby boy they called Tally, and the red-haired boy, who was called Hibbo. Paul had seen from his worksheet that his real name was Russell Hibbert. There was Art in the afternoon, and they painted a huge sign together for above the classroom door, saying: YEAR SIX. Hibbo was getting covered in paint. Paul had to keep remembering to answer to David, but apart from that, he was fine. By the end of the day, he had almost forgotten who he really was.

Real life crashed back in when hometime came. He had to get his blazer back, and go home. What would Masterville High have done, when he didn't turn up? Where was the real David Ashwood? Was he still playing snooker?

He didn't know the answers. He only knew he wanted this to go on. This had been the happiest day of his school life.

Before leaving the classroom, Hibbo said:

"See you tomorrow, Dave."

Paul waited until everyone else had gone, helping Miss Amari to tidy the paints and brushes away. She rewarded him with another smile. Then he slipped along to the cloakroom. His blazer and his bag were still where he had dropped them. He hid the blazer under the bag until he was across the yard, then once he was out in the street he put the blazer on and joined the back of the line of kids filing onto the Masterville High School bus. No one was paying any attention to him. He checked his reflection in the window. He must look neat and tidy for Nan.

She was waiting for him when he got in, and he didn't need his key. She was ready with another hug.

"So, my big boy's home! How was your day?"

He didn't need to answer. There was a big grin all over his face. His fears of the morning were long gone. He had beaten them, though not in the way he meant to.

Nan had chops and chips ready for their tea, and they sat and watched the soaps together, as they always did. She seemed a little surprised there was no homework. Paul brushed her worries aside.

"It starts tomorrow."

He would have to go upstairs to do some homework in future, whether Miss Amari set any or not. But Nan didn't ask any more questions. She kept saying:

"I'm so pleased you like the school."

Next morning, Paul was in his blazer again. He had to leave the house as Paul, before becoming David. But he needed something else, as well. Nan found him fetching his summer coat from the cupboard under the stairs.

"It was a bit chilly, in that yard."

The sun was shining, but Paul put the coat on, hiding his blazer. Then he went out and caught the bus. When they got to the schools, he slipped out and joined the younger kids heading for the First School.

The cloakroom gave some problems. He had to wait until he was alone, and with Hibbo and Salim and Tally all greeting him as an old friend, this was difficult. He made an excuse about going to the loo, and hid in there until they'd gone to the classroom. Then he slipped the coat and the blazer off and hung them up together, again using the coat to hide what was underneath. He felt like a superhero, assuming his secret identity.

Another brilliant day followed. He felt he'd been in this school all his life – or should have been. Occasionally he wondered about David Ashwood. There had been no sign of him at all, today. No worries. *He* was David Ashwood, now.

They did more Maths, and a History lesson on the Stone Age and the Iron Age. Again, they were topics Paul had done before, but Miss Amari made them new, and interesting, and fun. There was a school trip coming up, to the remains of a Roman amphitheatre. Paul had never done that before. In the afternoon they did P.E. and Miss Amari started with a very funny game that involved shaking themselves around and making silly noises. Hibbo and Tally were very good at silly noises, and Paul laughed until he thought his sides would split. The girls were giggling, and Paul felt quite pleased that they were there. Again, he thought how lucky he was. Other boys were next door in the Slammer, with that shouty man.

The trouble only began at the end of the day. Hibbo and the boys were gabbing away in the cloakroom, and Paul couldn't get a moment alone to rescue his blazer. Eventually Salim and Tally left, but Hibbo hung around. He had obviously appointed himself best mate to Paul – or David. He took his own coat from its peg, then before Paul could stop him, he took Paul's coat down as well, and chucked it to him.

"There you go, mate."

"Cheers." Paul took it, and tried to pretend he hadn't noticed the blazer. But Hibbo had.

"Hey, what's this doing here? It's one of them blazers from the Slammer."

"Someone must have left it here," said Paul. He looked nervously at Hibbo, as he reached out a freckled hand to the blazer. "Hey, you'd better leave it alone, Hibbo…"

Hibbo wasn't listening. He stroked the Masterville High School badge.

"Them Year Sevens are always playing pranks on us. One of their blazers… yeah? Right…"

He yanked at one of the buttons on the front of the blazer, pulling it straight off. Paul's eyes went massive.

"Hibbo!"

"Come off easy, don't they?" Hibbo was enjoying himself. He broke the stitches of the second button, then the third. He let all three buttons fall from his hand, down the back of the bench. "Let's leave 'em a little present, as well…"

He rummaged in his pockets, brought out a piece of very chewed gum in its wrapper, an apple core, and a huge ream of snotty toilet tissue. Paul began to realise his new friend wasn't the cleanest of boys.

He paled as Hibbo stuffed each of the items into a different blazer pocket.

"Serve 'em right." He gave Paul a friendly, but painful slap on the shoulder. "You coming to mine, tomorrow night? Get some food? The other guys will be there. 16 Barham Crescent."

"Thanks," whispered Paul. He gave a last, agonised look at his blazer – what was left of it. Nan would go mad.

There was nothing he could do but leave it there. He put his coat on over the grey jumper, then they set off across the yard. Hibbo was like a flaming torch, lighting their way. He was actually taller than Paul, despite being younger. It was ridiculous.

Paul took a nervous look towards the school bus.

"You going that way?" Hibbo asked. Paul nodded. "See you, then."

Paul breathed a sigh of relief as Hibbo made off across the Masterville Estate. It was lucky his friend was local. He noticed Barham Crescent, as the bus passed by. He had tea with Hibbo to look forward to. It was silly. David was now more popular than Paul had ever been.

He fastened up his coat, hoping Nan wouldn't see he had no blazer on. But when he entered the house, Nan seemed to have other things on her mind. She was on the phone.

"Listen, don't threaten me with court, missus, I was in the Wrens. Look, he's been there yesterday, and today. I know he has. You've got the wrong kid. Here he is now." She looked round, and covered the receiver with her hand. "It's your soft school. Say you never turned up yesterday, or today."

Paul went cold. Then he looked at the bag in his hand. He quickly opened it and started to unpack.

"He's showing me… yes, look, homework. History, by the look of it. And there's his wallet… dinner money, all spent… and… pooh, yes! There's his P.E. kit I'll have to wash. And you're telling me… well, check again! Yes! Thank you."

She put the phone down.

"Stupid people. Did you have a nice day? I don't know what those daft beggars are on about. You'd never play truant, would you?" She looked at Paul.

"You *were* in school, today, weren't you? Paul? Look me in the eye?"

Paul did.

"Yeah, Nan. I was in school today."

Nan relaxed.

"Yes, 'course you were. Now, you go and get changed. It's haddock goujons, for tea."

She went into the kitchen, and Paul shot off upstairs.

He was in trouble now. But what could he do? He didn't even know where the real David Ashwood was.

He changed into his own clothes, quickly did the History homework. Then they had their haddock goujons and watched the soaps. Nan was pleased when Paul told her about the invitation from Hibbo.

"I'm glad you're making friends. Is he in all your classes?"

"Yeah, yeah Nan. He is."

"Should ask him round here, one night."

"Oh." Paul was silent for a moment. "Thanks."

When he went to bed, he didn't feel as happy as the night before. What if Nan found out? What if the shouty man at Masterville found out?

And where on earth was David Ashwood?

The following morning, Paul put on what was left of his uniform. But Nan was getting ready to go out, as well. She had her coat and scarf on.

"I'll come with you, this morning. That bus goes on into Town. Do some shopping. You need new undies."

Paul went red, and not just at the last word. Nan looked at him.

"Where's your blazer?"

Paul's mouth went dry.

"I left it in school. After P.E."

"Well, that was daft, wasn't it? You get it back, first thing. That blazer cost a fortune."

Paul nodded, and tried not to think of what Hibbo had done to the blazer.

He felt a bit embarrassed on the bus, with Nan next to him, and all the other kids watching. Like someone was holding his hand.

When they reached the schools, he said goodbye. But the bus was still there, and Nan was still watching him.

He had no choice but to walk towards Masterville High, and join the other boys moving towards the entrance. He got in among some Year Tens and Elevens. They were taller, and made better cover.

He was running out of time to escape. Once he was through the high school doors, that would be it.

Please go, Nan! Please let that bus go!

He risked a look back.

The bus had finally moved on, taking Nan with it.

He made a dart for freedom, and pushed his way back, nearly knocking several Year Tens flying. Some very rude remarks followed him.

Then he ran for the First School.

In the cloakroom, he had to rummage down the back of the bench to find the missing buttons. There was no way to fix them back on. He took the blazer down, pulled all of Hibbo's disgusting rubbish out of the pockets, then ran into the loo to find a bin and a washbasin. He scrubbed his hands. Back outside, he hung the blazer up neatly again, and covered it with his coat. He hoped the other boys would leave it alone.

The danger seemed to have passed, and he had a Science lesson with Miss Amari on the Solar System, and roast gammon with roast potatoes for his lunch. It was strange. He now felt happier as David than he did as Paul. After another kickabout with the lads, they went on with their Iron Age project.

At the end of school, he remembered his promise to Nan. He had to go home later in that blazer. Hibbo gave him a look of surprise when he took it down.

"Hey, you're not really gonna nick it, are you?" He laughed as Paul put the blazer on over his jumper. "You are one crazy guy. Knew you'd be all right." He aimed a friendly punch at Paul. "You can pretend you're one of the big boys, now."

They went off together, onto the Estate, and made their way to Barham Crescent. Hibbo was walking along low walls… or backwards… anything not to be sensible.

His home and his Mum were as untidy and scruffy and kind and friendly as he was. Paul hid the blazer among a mess of coats and laundry that hung about the hall. There were newspapers and magazines spread all over the lounge, and unwashed pans on the kitchen table. Paul's Nan would have fainted if she'd seen the cooker. Thankfully, they were going out to eat. Salim and Tally came, and Hibbo's Mum took them for burgers and fries. Hibbo made them laugh by throwing fries in the air and catching them in his mouth.

Halfway through his veggieburger, Salim said:

"Hey, did you see the news before, Dave?"

Paul took a moment to remember his name. He shook his head.

"There's some lad, same name as you. He's in hospital. Got knocked down by a car, Monday afternoon. Hit and run. They're looking for the driver."

Paul choked on his orangeade. He struggled for breath. Hibbo started over-slapping him on the back.

"I was quite worried, when I heard David Ashwood. Same age as us, and everything. I thought maybe you'd had an accident after school. But then they said Monday, so…"

"Poor lad," said Hibbo's Mum. "But what was he doing out, on Monday afternoon, when he should've been in school? There's too many of these kids, bunking off. I blame the parents."

Paul managed to speak.

"Will he be OK?"

"He's in intensive care."

"That doesn't sound good," said Hibbo. He went on with his onion rings.

Paul left the rest of his meal uneaten.

He got the bus home shortly after eight. The evening was warm for September, and he felt very hot in coat, blazer, jumper and shirt.

He was forced to take the coat off and show the blazer to Nan. He muttered something about someone doing it in school, which was true.

"Little vandals," Nan said. "I thought this was meant to be a good school? Any more trouble, you tell me. I'll tell them where they get off. I've not forgotten that phone call yesterday. And they rang this morning. Their number was on 1471, when I got in. Well, they can stop phoning up with nonsense. I saw you go to school, myself."

She went to find a needle and thread, and Paul ran to his room. He lay face down on the bed. He was shaking.

He was thinking of the real David Ashwood, lying in hospital.

In the early hours of the morning, Paul knew he had to put this right. He had to go to his proper school, and tell the truth. He couldn't go on living his life a year behind. He would be twelve soon, while everyone thought he was ten or eleven. He would still be at school when others went to work or college. And surely someone must have told Masterville First School what had happened to the real David?

Paul had no energy left when seven o'clock came. It had all been used up in thinking and worrying. But somehow he managed to get up. Nan had left the blazer hanging on the front of his wardrobe, looking as good as new.

He couldn't eat his Instaporridge and fruit loaf. Nan

kept putting her hand on his forehead, asking him if he felt OK. He nodded.

When he took the bus, he truly meant to go into Masterville High, find the shouty man in room 37, confess.

Before he knew it, he was in the First School playground.

What could he do? He was going mad. He had to tell someone.

Miss Amari. She was kind. She would understand.

He opened the same door he had used on his first morning, went in. Automatically, he went into the cloakroom, dumped his coat and blazer.

The classroom was empty. He stood under their YEAR SIX sign, feeling like a fraud. Like a museum exhibit with the wrong label.

He looked at all the empty chairs. His friends sat here. He wanted to stay with them. All this was so unfair.

He jumped as he saw Miss Amari entering.

She wasn't her usual cheerful self. Her face was as worried as Paul's. But it cleared as she saw him.

"David! Then… oh, some people are really sick…"

She went to her desk, sank into her chair. She put a hand to her head.

Paul came nearer to her. He liked Miss Amari. "Are you OK, miss?"

"I've just had a bit of a shock, that's all." Miss Amari sounded bewildered. "I had to take a phone call, as Mrs Shaw's on a course…"

Paul knew by now that Mrs Shaw was the Head.

"It was someone claiming to be your Dad. They said… you'd had an accident… you were in hospital. But as you're obviously OK…"

Paul nodded.

"You live with your Nan, anyway, don't you? I remember, from your profile."

"Yes, miss," Paul said.

"Honestly…" Miss Amari shook her head. "What kind of person makes a prank call like that? To a school? About a boy your age? Anyway, I can see they were talking rubbish. Thank goodness!" She took a deep breath. "Saying you'd be off school for weeks…"

Paul knew he should be upset. And he hated to see Miss Amari like this. But there was a big grin, trying to break through his face.

David wouldn't be back for weeks! And Miss Amari, and therefore the school, still believed he was the real David Ashwood. He could stay here now!

Miss Amari was on her feet. She still looked a little shaken, but she had been a teacher for some time now. She knew how to get up and get on with it.

"You need to go out and line up with the rest. Sorry… did you want to see me about something?"

"No, miss." Paul was sliding towards the door. "It's fine."

Back outside in the yard, Paul let the grin appear. He'd won!

After all, it was everyone else's mistake. They all thought he was David. And David had never wanted to come to this school anyway. It served him right. It was Paul's school now. And this could last forever, if David died…

He caught his breath. He grabbed onto one of the playground benches for support. He couldn't believe that last thought. What *was* he turning into? Was he so afraid of the real world?

He felt Mum and Dad, looking down on him from Heaven, and was ashamed.

He wasn't stupid. He knew he was being selfish, and a coward. He had stolen David's life. And Masterville High would still be looking for Paul.

Unless…

Another selfish thought had entered his mind, and he couldn't get rid of this one. It was such a good idea… no, it was a *brilliant* idea. And it had come from Miss Amari.

He was thinking about it all through Maths. It didn't matter that he wasn't listening. He could still do the lesson. He'd done it twelve months previously.

At break-time, he declined to play football with Hibbo and the gang, told them he had a call to make. Phones weren't really allowed in school, but plenty of kids sneaked them in. His was in his top shirt pocket, under his jumper.

He went to the far corner of the yard, behind the Infants' eco-shelter. He knew Masterville High's number. Nan had had the prospectus on the coffee table all summer, for when her friends came round.

He rang the school office.

He'd done some Drama workshops at his old school, and he had a very good, deep, growly voice, which he'd used for playing a Giant. It almost sounded grown-up.

"Hi? Yes, it's Paul Marsh's Dad here. I'm sorry we didn't ring before, but we've been at the hospital all week. Paul's had an accident. He..." Better not make it too similar. "He fell off... a ladder, when he was helping me clean the windows. Yes, first floor. Straight onto concrete. He's broken a leg, and an arm. No, I don't think he'll be coming to your school for some time. I'm really sorry... No, his Nan didn't know. We didn't want to worry her. She's getting a bit confused..." He felt terrible, saying that about Nan. "But we've told her now. We'll keep you up to date..." He felt a sudden surge of nerves. "Yes, bye."

He hung up.

He couldn't believe it. He'd just put himself in hospital. Maybe he could visit David.

He walked across the yard. There was no going back now. There was no Paul Marsh, anymore. Just David Ashwood.

While Paul lay in hospital, David painted a solar system in ping-pong balls, and ate pasta, peas and bacon and a cookie, and listened to their class reader, and felt wonderful. And the next day was just as good. At the weekend he went bowling with Hibbo and Salim and Tally, and killed himself laughing when Tally lost his balance and nearly bowled himself after the ball. On Monday evening he had a trial for the school football team, and was swiftly signed. On Tuesday evening he went to their Drama Club. The class had come completely to accept him as a friend, and he got on with everyone. He didn't even need to worry about the blazer anymore. Hibbo and the gang now thought he was a crazy rebel who liked coming to school in the big boys' uniform, just to show how hard he was. And Nan had no more phone calls. He was going home with a big smile on his face, and eating every scrap of his meals. Nan was soon telling her friends how well Paul had settled in to big school.

The second week of term soon passed, and then the third. Paul hadn't thought about David Ashwood or Masterville High for days. There were now far more people calling him David than Paul, and at home there were moments when he forgot to answer to his real name. He felt far happier as David. Masterville First School was where he belonged.

In week four of term he went on the amphitheatre trip, and bought Nan a little model of a gladiator for their mantelpiece. She had given him the money for the trip, and had no idea it was Year Six History, rather than Year Seven. The online consent form had been a worry, but Paul tipped the screen of her ageing laptop so that the light shone upon it, and hid her glasses. She had no idea who the email was from, or whose website they had linked to. Paul had set up an email account, and given its address to the First School. He checked it every evening.

He had been for tea with Hibbo three times now and really wanted to invite him back. He was on a roll. He could face the fear. He arranged tea for Friday evening, and briefed Hibbo that same afternoon.

"By the way, my Nan calls me Paul, not David. It's my middle name. So that's why. Come over about six." That way, they would both have time to get changed, and there could be no uniform questions. "She knows all the school news too, so no need to tell her anything."

Hibbo arrived at twenty to seven, in a violent orange tracksuit to match his hair, with gleaming white trainers and a ring that looked as if a chocolate coin was stuck to his finger. Nan's eyes bulged slightly when she saw him. But she cooked them fish fingers, chips and mushy peas, and gave them the little dining-room to themselves, while she had peace and quiet and fish pie in the kitchen. Paul was glad they didn't have to get through a whole meal with her. Hibbo was behaving himself quite well, but made a right mess of mopping up his mushy peas with his bread, and was burping louder than Paul thought strictly necessary. After tea they played with Paul's games console.

It was only when Hibbo was leaving that things became awkward. Nan came out into the hall to see him off.

"It's been nice meeting you, Russell. I'm so pleased Paul's made friends."

Hibbo looked at Paul, and wisely gave a wink.

"I was so worried about him going on to big school."

Paul kicked the radiator suddenly, but too late. Hibbo seemed a little puzzled as he looked at Paul.

"It's a bigger school than your last one, is it?"

"Oh, yes," Nan went on. "He used to be just up the road from here."

"But I thought you just moved here?"

"Oh, no. He's lived round here all his life."

"So why'd you come to our school?"

Nan laughed. "Well, he's a bit old for the other one, now, isn't he?" She passed Hibbo his coat. It had a designer label. "Thank you for looking after him so well."

"Nan! I'm not five!"

"No, I mean it. He had a bit of a rough start, didn't you, love? Some little yobbo pulled the buttons off his blazer."

Hibbo gave Paul a very funny look.

They were interrupted by a car horn outside. Hibbo's Dad had arrived to collect him. Paul opened the front door, a bit too eagerly.

"See you for football tomorrow, then?"

Hibbo was already over the step.

"See you, Dave!"

Nan closed the door.

"*Dave?*"

A ghastly grin crossed Paul's face.

"It's… a nickname. Street talk… slang. When you've got a best mate, you… call him Dave. Like… Buddy. Sort of thing. Thanks for tea, Nan… great. He's a nice lad, isn't he? Think I'll have an early night. Bye."

He shot off upstairs, leaving Nan staring after him.

Paul was lucky that another weekend followed. Hibbo lived very much in the moment, and the next day his head was full of their football team. By Monday he had forgotten the strange conversation with Paul's Nan. Paul realised he'd better not take the lads home again. Not yet, anyway. They could go out to places...

They were now in week five. Only three weeks until half-term. Paul couldn't believe he was still getting away with it. There had been no more from Masterville High. No more word of David. Paul hoped he was all right. Paul might have been the world's youngest identity thief, but he still had a heart.

Then on Wednesday morning, Miss Amari made the announcement.

"I've got some exciting news for you all... on Friday, we're making a special visit to Masterville High, and we're going to have a High School Experience Day."

Paul went pale.

"It'll give some of you boys a taste of where you'll be in a year's time. And the rest of you will find out what a secondary school's like, ahead of Induction next July. Now, we had to do this when the teacher was free, so there isn't much time. There's an email going out this afternoon. Will all of you get your parents or guardians to do the consent form tonight, and we'll go next door at half nine on Friday morning. Don't bring lunch, anyone, we're getting it there..."

Paul didn't hear a word she said for the rest of the lesson. He couldn't go. They might recognise him. He couldn't let Nan fill the consent form in... he couldn't let her see the email at all. But someone had to do it. If the school didn't get the OK, Miss Amari would want to know why. He couldn't stay at the First School on Friday, all on his own.

There was only one thing for it. He went and found the laptop as soon as he got home, logged in and did the consent form himself. Luckily, Nan was upstairs changing the beds. When Friday came, he would pretend to be ill, and award himself the day off. There were some nasty bugs, going around school...

He was becoming more like David Ashwood every day.

On Friday morning he was ready to overheat the thermometer and groan, but Nan never gave him the chance. She was into his room, undrawing the curtains, pulling back his duvet to eject him from the bed.

"Come on, love. I need you to make an early start this morning. Come on, I'm getting the bus with you. I need to go to the building society, and there's a sale on at Bentley's..."

Paul was up, showered, dressed and breakfasted before he knew what had hit him. He looked at his blazer in the hall mirror. He would really have to lose it today. He couldn't go into Masterville High in their uniform!

He was longing to run, but Nan was by his side all the way, from home to bus-stop to the schools. It was like that first Wednesday again. Luckily, the bus went quickly, and he didn't have to enter the High School. But he would be there soon...

He couldn't bunk off now. There were too many of his classmates around. And he didn't want to get knocked down by a car, like the real David.

He went on into the First School, trying to keep calm. Probably hardly anyone at the High School knew what he looked like. They all thought Paul Marsh was in hospital, or getting better at home. He would be one face in a crowd of kids. Wherever they went, he would sit at the back. He would keep completely quiet, and his head down...

He dumped the blazer, then went to their classroom. It was buzzing. Girls and boys alike were excited about a morning at big school.

Miss Amari did a quick register, then she and a teaching assistant led everyone out of the front entrance and along the road to Masterville High. Paul walked with Hibbo and Salim and Tally. He felt an odd feeling of coldness. A sense of impending doom. Like a walk to a death cell.

He found himself in the High School's reception, with the whole class looking around and upward, as if surprised by how high the ceilings were. He felt a little happier when he saw the teacher who had come to meet them. He was youngish, with brown curly hair, a fresh-coloured face and a superhero smile. He was obviously a P.E. teacher, with his dark blue tracksuit jacket, and shorts that revealed very hairy legs.

"Morning, everyone. I'm Mr Jay. I'm one of the Year Seven form teachers this year. And I do Geography, and P.E. So, here's how it works. We'll go on up to my form room, I'll tell you a bit about high school life, then one of our Year Seven students will come and talk to you. Right team, wagons roll..."

They followed him along the corridors. Miss Amari and the assistant were coming too. Paul frowned. He seemed to know this route.

They were going upstairs…

He was feeling fainter. He did know this route, and this corridor. The classroom they were going to… out of all the rooms in this huge building… it couldn't be…

It was.

Mr Jay unlocked the door to room 37. Year Six started streaming in.

"David?" Miss Amari was looking at Paul. He wasn't moving. "What's wrong?"

Paul avoided her eye. Slowly, he moved forward and through the dreaded door.

He was surprised to enter a brightly-lit classroom that looked much larger and more modern than their room at the First School. There was a colourful display of Geography work along one wall, and another display opposite headed *GCSE PE*. At the front were big posters of *Star Mission* and *Captain Nine*. Mr Jay was obviously a big kid at heart.

This couldn't be his room…? Where was the shouty man? Paul was sure it hadn't been Mr Jay's voice, on that first morning…

In a daze, he sat at a desk and began to listen.

Mr Jay started talking about Masterville High, and was full of funny stories, some his own, some from other teachers, about kids getting lost on Orienteering and tents falling down on camping trips and the lights failing in the school play. He made secondary school sound cool. The class seemed to like him. So did Miss Amari, watching from the back of the room.

Paul didn't get this at all. If this would have been his form room… then Mr Jay would have been…

There was a knock at the door.

"Come!" Mr Jay called.

The door opened to reveal a stocky, thick-set boy with dark hair. He looked about Paul's age.

"Ah, there you are." Mr Jay beckoned the boy over. "Year Six, this is one of my Year Sevens. Now – do you want to introduce yourself?"

The boy stepped forward.

"Hi. I'm Paul Marsh."

Paul sat up very straight in his seat.

He must be dreaming. He couldn't really be here… but the uncomfortable chair felt real. So did the sweat breaking out on his back.

The other Paul was grinning.

"Actually, I nearly never made it to this school. I had an accident, just before term started. Fell off a ladder. Ended up in hospital. But I'm all right now. And I'm really enjoying Masterville High."

Behind his desk, Paul's eyes were growing bigger, and bigger, and bigger.

"I didn't tell him to say that, honest," said Mr Jay. The Year Sixes tittered. "Well, we're very pleased to have you, Paul. So tell us – did you find it scary, starting big school?"

"Oh, yeah," said the other Paul. "First day, I didn't know the school…I couldn't find my way. But then I did, and everything's great now."

"Must admit," said Mr Jay. "I missed *my* first week, too. Came back from holiday with a nasty bug. So my poor form had a supply teacher, for week one. But I met them in week two, and we get on fine. And you're my right-hand man, Paul Marsh. Aren't you?"

Paul was staring at them. He found himself rising slowly to his feet. Hibbo and the other kids turned to look at him in surprise. He was raising his hand, pointing towards the other Paul.

Mr Jay looked surprised, too. "Did you want something?"

"He's…" Paul was fighting to speak. "I'm…"

"David?" Miss Amari came down the room. "We're guests, here. I hope you're not going to misbehave." She looked at Mr Jay. "This is David Ashwood. He's usually *my* right-hand man."

"You're…" Paul found breath. "You're not Paul Marsh!"

The other Paul grinned. "No? Who am I, then? Durwyn the Dragon?"

"You can't be!"

"And why not?"

"Because…" Paul paused. "Because *I* am!"

"David?" Miss Amari still sounded puzzled. "What do you mean? You're David Ashwood, Year Six, Masterville First School. Aren't you?" She looked at the rest of her class. "Isn't he?"

"YES!" everyone shouted.

"Paul's a Year Seven," said Mr Jay. "He's a much bigger boy than you. You're only… what… eleven? Ten?"

"I'm nearly twelve!" Paul came to the front of the room. He searched his pockets, found his school travel pass. "Look – here's my name, and when I was born."

Mr Jay reached out a massive hairy hand and took it.

"Paul Marsh... born 29th October, two thousand and..." He looked at Paul. His eyes were full of mischief. "Well, well. So you are."

The other Paul was moving across the room. He opened the form room door again.

The teaching assistant entered. Paul hadn't noticed her absence until now.

And with her was Paul's Nan.

She didn't seem to be enjoying the joke quite as much. Her eyes were narrow as she looked at her grandson and said:

"Hello, David."

"We found out three days ago," said Miss Amari, later that morning. They were all downstairs, in the school's canteen, getting an early lunch. There were sandwiches and sausage rolls and samosas. But Paul wasn't eating. Around him were Miss Amari and Mr Jay and Nan. "David Ashwood's Dad rang the school again. David's lucky. He's getting better. It *was* his Dad, the first time, wasn't it? Paul?"

Paul couldn't look at her. He nodded.

"*We* were getting worried about Paul Marsh," said Mr Jay. "So we sent a letter home. Your Nan rang us up. I've been trying to work out how a boy can be here and not here. Your Nan said you'd been out in your blazer every morning. We had to bring you out of hiding somehow." He pointed to the stocky boy, who had his face around a sausage roll. "So we got Logan over there to stand in for you."

He was grinning, but Miss Amari looked more sympathetic.

"Poor you. Were you really so scared, of big school?"

"I…" Paul swallowed. "I couldn't find the room, and then I heard the supply teacher shouting…"

"Yeah…" Mr Jay said. "I heard he was a bit of a gorilla."

"So I ran for it, and went next door. I never meant to lie… but…" He looked at the teachers. "You know what happened… with my Mum and Dad? And I was missing my old school. I've felt so happy, in Miss Amari's class…" He stopped. "So what happens now? Sir? Miss?"

"I dunno," said Mr Jay. "Normally when kids bunk off school, the parents or guardians get into trouble… but you've been in school every day! Just the wrong one. We'll have to wait and see what happens…"

Very quickly, he gave Paul a wink. Paul suddenly felt hopeful.

Then he looked around and saw his classmates, eating and drinking and laughing. He looked back at Miss Amari.

"I suppose I can't come back with you?"

"We all have to grow up sometime, Paul," Miss Amari said. She smiled. "I hope you'll come back and see us, though. We'll need someone to come into *our* school next, tell us more about big school! It's usually someone who left the year before. This time, it'll be someone the class all know! And I don't think Russell lets friends go that easily…"

Mr Jay gave another grin.

"Come on, bro. Man up. And after lunch I'll take you to meet your real form. They all want to see Paul Marsh, Man of Mystery! Your name's been on the register since the start of term. You're famous! You'll have thirty new mates, by hometime."

He went off to talk to the other Year Sixes, and Miss Amari went with him. Nan gave Paul a look.

"You just wait 'til I get you home. *Confused…!*"

Paul slunk away from her. He went to join Hibbo, who was looking very confused himself.

"So… you're Paul?"

"Yeah."

"So… who's David?"

"David's in hospital. But he'll be OK. You can meet him, soon."

"So… who's…?"

"That's Logan."

"So who am I?"

"You're still Hibbo."

"Right." Hibbo shook his fiery head. "You are one crazy guy." He dug Paul's arm with his fist. "Miss you, Dave. Hey, you coming out for burgers again? Tomorrow?"

Paul gave him a friendly dig in return.

"Yeah. I could ask Logan, too. Get all the Pauls together."

Hibbo grinned. He went over to Salim and Tally.

Paul took a deep breath. He looked around, at his old school and his new school. He looked from his old teacher to his new teacher. Then he went to Mr Jay.

It was only then that he remembered his blazer.

It was still at the First School.

A School Knight

Myra first saw Shane one chilly January morning, on the bus into school.

She was sitting by the grubby window, alone as usual, as houses and trees and vehicles and the community centre flashed by. Beside her on the seat was a bag that contained a plastic tub that contained packages that contained everything you needed to make cinnamon flapjacks. She had her hands through the handles of the bag. She didn't have Food Tech until this afternoon, but she wasn't letting the bag out of her sight. Last time some of the boys had got hold of it, and swapped all her ingredients with those from other bags, throwing in a plastic tarantula for good measure. Idiots.

The girls were no better. Myra's friends Aisha and Evie had gone to Grammar School, and if she had got one per cent more on the Eleven Plus, Myra would have been there too. Instead she was at Sansford High, where Lara and her gang of girls mocked and picked on Myra because she sounded posher than them, and lived on the May View Estate, and did her work and was polite to teachers. It was now quite clear to Myra that she wasn't cool or pretty, and never would be cool

136

or pretty, and would spend the next five years with a target painted on the front of her uniform blouse.

The bus made its last stop before reaching the school. Myra saw several of the older kids getting on. That was another reason she hated secondary school. It was Big School, and Myra had always been small for her age. When Years Ten and Eleven appeared, it was like World of the Giants.

Look at this boy. He was so tall he nearly reached the roof of the bus, a young man exploding out of a schoolboy's uniform. He had to be Year Eleven. Myra looked upwards. He had black hair and a tanned, nut-brown face, and his tie was crooked. He was wearing a gold signet ring, and black trousers instead of grey, and white trainers, totally ignoring the school uniform rules.

He chucked his bag down with a *thump!* and sat on the seat alongside hers, stretching out his incredibly long legs in front of him. He seemed to be all arms and legs, which ended in very big hands and feet.

Suddenly he saw her. His wide brown eyes gave her a curious look. Without stopping to think, Myra smiled.

She blushed as he smiled back. He had a wide, cheeky grin that showed perfect white teeth.

She quickly turned away, staring out of the window again. When she was sure enough time had passed, she had another look. He had turned to his window as well. There was condensation, and he was idly drawing patterns in it with a long, brown finger, as if he were a little boy.

Myra sat watching him for the rest of the journey.

She wasn't sure why, but he kept coming back to her thoughts for the whole of the school day. He was there while she was doing fractions and percentages. He was there in her tuna jacket potato. He was there in Food Tech, and she nearly burnt the flapjacks, and poured water all up her sleeve while doing the washing-up. Lara and the other girls giggled at her.

She found herself running for the bus, clutching her satchel and the plastic bag, the tub of flapjacks bumping against her leg. She wondered if he would be there…

She seemed to be out of luck. She went along the whole lower deck, ignoring several seats she could have taken. She might have known she'd never see him again.

Then she went up the stairs to the top deck, and there he was, again seated beside a window, and fiddling with his shiny silver phone. Thumb thumb thumb thumb thumb… She could see he was a bit of a fidget.

It was quieter, up here. There was a space beside him. Myra fought a quick battle with herself. *Go on Myra.* No don't, you're tiny to him! He'll think you're mad. *But he smiled at you. Go on, go on…*

She was sitting next to him before she even realised.

He looked up from the phone.

In a very high-pitched voice, Myra said:

"Hi."

"Hey." The big boy gave her another friendly smile. Myra felt herself going red again. He looked pleased to see her – which was rare at this school – and not at all surprised. He had a husky voice that had almost finished going down, and was stuck somewhere around the first floor. "How are you?"

"Yeah!" Myra nodded enthusiastically. "I'm fine."

"Good."

They were silent for a few moments. Myra had no idea what to say. She felt like a pixie trying to talk to a giant. Her guilty secret was that she still enjoyed reading fairy tales, and she had a big, colourful, illustrated book of them hidden under her bed at home. Actually, he wasn't the giant. He looked more like the Prince on page 47.

He seemed to sense her shyness. He offered a massive hand, turned sideways for a street handshake.

"I'm Shane."

"I'm Myra." Myra's hand almost disappeared into his. It felt nice and warm, on this cold afternoon. She fought to think of something else to say. "Nice ring."

"Oh, ta." Shane turned his hand again, so that the ring caught the light. "I keep getting told to take it off. So I just flip it from one hand to the other. See?" He switched the ring to his left hand. "Then I make sure the teachers only see one hand at a time."

He was half-smiling, but his eyes looked serious. Myra had no idea if he was joking or not. She liked him, though. For the first time, someone at this school was treating her as a friend.

Shane drummed his fingers on the lid of the plastic tub.

"What you got there?"

"Been baking," Myra said. After a moment, she lifted the lid. "Would you like one? They're cinnamon."

"Oh, ta." Shane reached for the flapjacks. Some of them were sticking together. He prised one free, and took a bite. A small piece fell down, and he grabbed it with his other hand. "Mmm. They taste great. You one of them Great British Bakers?"

Myra giggled.

"You having one as well?"

"Oh. Oh, yeah." Myra took another flapjack and started to eat it. Shane was right. They did taste good.

Shane leaned back lazily against the seat, and continued to eat.

"Wasn't even gonna take the bus today. But I've left me bike somewhere, and I can't remember where. I was just messaging round, seeing if anyone's seen it."

"You can't remember where you put your own bike?"

"Got a busy life. I must've parked it, then walked home. Dunno what I'll be like when I get a car. Anyway, that's for next year. You first year?" Myra nodded. "How's big school, then?"

"It's OK. I wish I had more friends here."

"You sound too clever for this place."

"I am. Oh… present company excepted, of course." Shane laughed. "I don't fit in. Even the teachers seem to think I'm weird."

"You think you got problems? I was already five foot nine, when I was eleven. Nearly six five, now. I don't fit in school photos, anymore."

"I think it's very nice, being tall."

"Not when it's raining. It hits you first."

Myra smiled. She loved the way he said things like that. She was beginning to wish she was in Year Eleven.

She looked out of the window, as the bus drew to a halt.

"Isn't this your stop?"

"Sometimes," said Shane. "But tonight I'm going on. Someone needs me."

"What, secret mission?"

"Something like that." Shane turned his head towards two more big boys who were getting off the bus, a blond guy and a dark-haired guy. "Hey."

"New girlfriend, Shane?" The dark boy grinned. "They're getting younger."

Shane laughed. "Get out of here."

"She can cook, too," the blond boy said.

Myra made a grab for the flapjacks, as the blond boy snatched one. His friend followed suit.

"OI!" Shane bellowed. "Where's your manners, guys?"

The boys went down the steps, munching and grinning. Shane gave Myra an apologetic look.

"Sorry 'bout that. That's John, and Eddy. Right pair of jokers. But they're OK."

Myra quickly put the lid onto the tub and covered it with the bag. At this rate, there would be no flapjacks left for Mum or Nan! She wouldn't mind giving another one to Shane, though.

She felt thrilled, as the bus moved on. She would be with Shane for a bit longer, if he wasn't getting off.

He was too good at listening. She ended up telling him *everything*... about Lara and the bullies in her form... about missing her Dad since he ran off with the receptionist from his dentist's... about Mum working late at the hospital, and Nan coming over to look after her. Shane seemed to understand everything. Then he told her about himself. He lived with his Mum and Dad and big sister (Myra wondered how *anyone* could be bigger than Shane) and loved football and running and cycling, and hated school as much as Myra, and would be leaving in July and doing a Modern Apprenticeship. He wanted to be an electrician.

"I'm good with me hands. And I love me gadgets. If you ever want anything fixing..."

Myra made a note to break something, so he could fix it.

In the end, they both got off on the May View Estate. Shane nodded his head to her. It was almost a bow.

"Nice talking to you, Myra."

Myra felt a sudden panic that he was going away. This was ridiculous. She had only known him for half an hour.

"See you tomorrow?"

"Sure thing." Shane gave her a wink, a grin, and then his long legs led him away. Myra saw him take out his phone again, answer it. "Yeah? Yeah, no worries. I'll be there."

Myra was surprised to find it was still only four o'clock. She seemed to have been talking to Shane for ages.

Mum was working until seven, so Nan was there to prepare Myra's tea. They had macaroni cheese and vegetables and what was left of the flapjacks, setting a couple aside for Mum. Then Myra did her homework, evaluating them. They watched old comedy shows on Throwback until Mum came home.

All the time, Myra was thinking about Shane... the way he winked at her... his grin... the funny things he said.

She had never felt like this about a boy before, let alone a boy so big. Boys usually annoyed her. But Shane seemed really grown up.

Before going to bed, she pulled out the book of fairy tales, and sat looking at page 47 and the tall, tanned, handsome Prince.

The next morning she was first in the queue for the school bus. But there was no sign of Shane. Myra went up to the top deck, sat in the same seat, which she now thought of as their seat. She put her satchel down beside her, so no one else would sit there. She sat looking out of the window again, as the bus made another stop, then another. Where was he?

Then everything went dark. She realised someone had placed a pair of big brown hands over her eyes. Beneath them, Myra's mouth smiled.

"Hi, Shane!"

A grinning Shane came from the seat behind.

"Now, how d'you know it was me...?"

Myra moved the satchel so he could sit down. He was naughty... and like everyone else, he teased her... but with him, it was OK.

"Where did you spring from?"

"Stayed with a friend last night," said Shane. He reached into the pocket of his enormous school blazer and brought out a package wrapped in tinfoil. He opened it to reveal two thick slices of wholewheat toast, smothered with raspberry jam. "Breakfast?"

Myra had already had breakfast, but was quite happy to have another one with Shane. She took a slice, sank her teeth into it, and nearly didn't get them out again. It was like one of Nan's cork tablemats. She had a feeling Shane might have sat on it, as well. But the jam was nice. She was getting the seeds stuck in her teeth.

Shane chomped his way through, making his hands sticky. Then he pointed jammily towards John and Eddy, who were sitting further along the top deck, talking and laughing. They looked like they were hatching some plan.

"See those two? You know they used to bully me? First and second year?"

"You?"

"Oh yeah, tall guys get bullied too. They used to call me Lanky Legs, or Grasshopper. But now we respect each other. Know why?"

Myra shook her head.

"You saw it last night. I talked back to them. Fought fire with fire. I learnt not to get beaten down by them. Whatever they said, I had a comeback. You try that. Little by little. See where it gets you with those li'l boys and girls in your form. Yeah?"

Myra nodded. She finished the toast… somehow. Shane gave her a smile.

"Good girl."

Myra tried his advice that day, and it worked. When Lara said:

"Had your hair done, Myra? No? Thought not."

Myra came back with:

"Yours'll look better next week. You know, when it's blonde again?"

and two of the other girls actually laughed. After that, Lara left Myra alone for the whole day.

She saw Shane at lunchtime, kicking a ball around with John and Eddy and some other big people. She gave him a little wave, and he stopped playing long enough to give her a half-salute.

Their chats became a regular thing, after that. Shane wasn't always on the bus, sometimes taking a different one, sometimes cycling in – he seemed to have found his bike. He had a lot of calls and messages as well, but the rest of the time he was there for Myra. She talked to him about school worries (Lara, the boys, teachers) and home worries (Mum's stressful job as a nurse, Nan's arthritis, missing Dad) and he always had something sympathetic to say. She even enjoyed his teasing her. When he saw she enjoyed the 'eyes' gag he kept sneaking up and doing it, and Myra became used to the lights going out. He would hide her satchel under the seat, or slip things into her pocket for her to find later… a chocolate bar or a wrapped piece of chewing gum. Sometimes people on the bus would stare at them, but Myra didn't care. Shane was her friend.

One February morning at school, things went disastrously wrong for Myra. They had Geography with Mr Barber, with homework to hand in, and half the class had only done exercises 1 and 2, not 3 – including Myra. She was sure he had never said to do exercise 3, and half the class agreed with her, and so did her homework diary. When Mr Barber started giving out lunchtime detentions, she was honest enough to admit that she hadn't done that exercise either. Then Mr Barber gave a bellow.

"WHOA! Myra! Even Little Miss Perfect Myra hasn't done her work! Well, you can come back at lunchtime as well, and do some LINES!"

The whole class laughed, especially Lara and her gang, and Myra wanted to sink through the floor and disappear.

When lunchtime came, she was the only one who turned up for the detention. Mr Barber again bellowed her name, this time all along the corridor, and all the passing first-years laughed. Myra went in and wrote her lines for fifteen minutes. Her lip was trembling. She always did her work. She was sure he hadn't mentioned exercise 3. She had never had a detention before…

When the detention was over, she ran out into the yard, round the back of the Drama studio, and cried her eyes out. Mr Barber was horrible! This school was horrible! She couldn't take it, anymore! She was as clever as Aisha and Evie! Why couldn't she be with them?

She was in sight of the playing field outside the boys' gym, where Shane played football. When he saw her crying, he was over there in ten seconds flat. His long legs certainly came in useful.

"Flippin' heck... what's happened?"

Myra told him, through the sobs, and Shane's face became very angry, and he said in a very few words what he thought of Mr Barber. Then he opened his arms wide.

"D'you wanna hug?"

Myra stared at him. Then she nodded.

She stepped forward, and had the biggest, warmest, loveliest bear-hug she had ever had. Being wrapped up in Shane felt good. He was very strong. There was a friendly smell about him, which Myra liked... a mixture of cheap deodorant, school blazer and the pizza he must have had for lunch.

Nobody male except Dad had ever cuddled her...

She had stopped crying long before Shane let her go. Not having a handkerchief, he brushed her tears away with his hand.

He suddenly seemed to notice the way she was looking up at him. Awkwardly, he put out his finger and beeped her nose. A big grin spread across Myra's face, as if he had found the Smile Button.

"Better?"

"Better," Myra said.

Shane smiled. He patted her on the back, then disappeared back towards the playing field.

Myra didn't care about *anything*, anymore. She turned and ran back towards the school. She felt incredibly snug and safe and loved. Shane must have the magic touch.

She went into the form room and glared so fiercely at Lara and the others that no one dared to tease her about the detention.

Shane had saved her, again.

She was thinking about him all afternoon. When they got the bus home together, they were quieter than usual, looking awkwardly at each other, before finally they smiled. They couldn't say much with other kids listening, but finally Myra mouthed:

Thank you!

After a while, people took no further notice of them. Then, from his pocket, Shane took a rather leaky black ballpoint pen. Myra blinked.

"What are you doing?" She giggled as the back of her hand tickled. "Hey... don't write on me!"

She looked down. There was a mobile number on her hand. Shane pointed to it.

"My number. 'Case you need me."

He grinned.

"I'm always on duty."

As soon as she got in, Myra transferred the number into her phone. She sent a text to Shane, just saying *Thank you*, so he would have her number too. Then she went and scrubbed her hands. She had to get rid of this. She looked like a prisoner.

It wouldn't come off!

"Whose is that number?" Mum asked. It was her day off, and she had made spaghetti carbonara for them both. Myra was busy trying to lower it into her mouth, instead of her ear.

"A friend of mine from school," Myra said.

"Glad you're making friends," Mum said. "I was a bit worried you going there, without Aisha and Evie. Is it that nice girl Lara, who helped at Parents' Evening?"

"No, no Mum. It's not."

"You should do something together," Mum said. "Go out somewhere, on Saturday. A safe environment." There were times when Mum talked a bit too much like a health professional. "How about the Discovery Centre? I've got a shift, Saturday afternoon, but I could drop you off, then pick you up later. They've got a cafe. There's a new exhibition on dinosaurs…"

Myra wasn't the least bit interested in dinosaurs. But her face lit up.

"Yeah!"

On the bus next morning, Shane gave Myra his curious look.

"Did you just ask me out?"

Myra smiled, and went pink again. Shane seemed to be very good at making her change colour. She was quite the chameleon.

"There's an exhibition on dinosaurs. And there's all kinds of interactive stuff in the Discovery Centre... machines... gadgets. You'd love it. We could have lunch..." She saw the way Shane was looking at her. "Just friends."

"Oh, oh yeah," Shane said. "Just friends."

"I could meet you there at one..."

The bus was arriving at school. Shane's phone rang.

"I'll text you." He headed for the lower deck, answering the phone. "Yup?"

Myra stayed in her seat for a moment, still smiling to herself.

Phones weren't allowed in school, and she had to wait until break, and go behind the Drama studio again. Then she checked for messages. There was a text from Shane that said:

OK cu Sat 1pm.

Myra gave a little leap.

Saturday came, and Myra spent all morning looking for something to wear. She liked to look smart, but had never been this fussy about clothes before. In the end she settled on smart dark trousers and a white top with a pattern embossed in gold. She had a white baseball cap to match.

"You look very smart, for a museum," Mum said. "What's she called, this friend of yours?"

Myra's heart did a somersault.

"Shayyy... Shaw... Shaw... *Shona!* Shona."

Mum laughed.

"Now say that with your teeth in."

"Shona."

"I'm sorry I've got to work today," Mum said. She gave Myra £10. "That's for your lunch. I mean, the money's to buy lunch, don't eat it. There's a gift shop, too."

"Thank you!" Myra said. She hated hiding the truth from Mum. But after all, it wasn't everyone in Year Seven who had a secret boyfriend.

She went back to her room twice, to put perfume on, and to brush her hair again. On the second visit, she quickly took out the book and looked at the handsome Prince of page 47. Then she ran downstairs to Mum.

Mum dropped her right at the entrance to the Discovery Centre, gave her a wave, and waited until she had gone inside. Then Myra walked across the foyer. A T-Rex gazed sternly down at her. Myra gave it a guilty look.

"I've only come to meet a friend."

This place was very busy on a Saturday lunchtime, but there was no sign of Shane. Myra's heart was heading for her trainers. Perhaps he'd changed his mind...

Then, all at once, he was there, dressed in jeans and a striped top in red, blue and green. Combined with his height, it made him very easy to spot.

"Hey. Sorry I'm late. Had another mission to fulfil."

Myra knew he was a superhero, so didn't question this. She wanted to hug him, but there were too many people around.

"Do you want to go and get some lunch first? Then we can have a look around."

Shane gave her a thumbs-up. They went off together to find the cafe.

They queued at the counter. There was chilli con carne for Myra and an enormous fillet of fish with chips and mushy peas for Shane. He had a can of orangeade and Myra chose an iced tea. At the till, Shane shook his head when he saw Myra's £10 note.

"I'll get these. Been working. I mended Mrs Lewis's kettle. She's next door to us."

"I'll get the drinks?"

"No, don't be daft." Shane paid before Myra could say any more. The woman behind the till smiled.

"Looks after you, does he? Your big brother?"

"Yeah." Myra giggled. "He does." She turned to Shane. "Come on. Bro."

They went together to a table by the window. Shane sniggered.

"Flippin' heck. First we're going out, now we're family."

"I always wanted a brother," said Myra. Shane smiled.

He had a healthy appetite, as usual, and soon the fish was only skin and bone. Myra was too excited to finish her chilli. What would the girls at school think? First date at only eleven. So much for Lara and her fancy hairstyles.

After lunch they had a walk around the dinosaurs, and then went into the Egyptian Zone, where there were mummies and model pyramids. She loved being with Shane, though he was the sort of person *Do Not Touch* signs are made for, and she couldn't stop him touching and prodding and poking things. She led him into the Science Zone, which had lightning globes and model solar systems where you could move the planets, and a green-screen flying carpet, and lots of dials to turn and buttons to press. He could fiddle about in there to his heart's content. He looked more excited than some of the smaller boys who were here.

They reached a wind tunnel… a vertical shaft with a strong current of air circulating inside. There were little pieces of confetti blowing around, to show the direction of the current.

Myra saw Shane's eyes gleam. He gave her a mischievous look. Then he snatched the cap from her head and chucked it into the column.

"What? Noooo!" Myra was too late to save the cap. She watched it spinning round and round in there, like a satellite orbiting a planet. She tried to grab it back, but it was out of reach, being sucked higher and higher into the tunnel. "Shane! You…!"

She suddenly realised there was someone standing behind them. Two people.

She turned, and saw a familiar figure standing next to a young blonde woman with gleaming teeth.

Slowly, Myra said:

"Oh. Hi, Dad."

"Myra…" said Dad. He looked at his companion. "This is Carrie. From…"

"The dentist, yeah." Myra turned to Shane, trying to ignore the cap still flying around nearby. "This is Shane… from…"

"Hi," said Shane uncomfortably.

Myra suddenly felt far too small.

"So… did you enjoy the dinosaurs?"

"That was so embarrassing," Shane said in the foyer. Myra was still capless, and her heart was thumping. "What if he tells your Mum?"

"She's not talking to him. Anyway, it's OK. Just friends."

"Oh yeah. Just friends."

Myra stuck her lower lip out.

"They're not going to spoil my day. I mean, our day. If Dad can bring his girlfriend, then I can bring my… just friend. Now, let's go to the gift shop. I want to buy you a rocket."

"Oh, cheers."

"Despite the fact that you're an evil boy who sent my favourite cap into space!"

"Ha!"

They went into the gift shop, and Myra kept her promise. The rocket was a kit that came in several pieces. Myra bought a new cap – a red one with DISCOVERY CENTRE on it. Thankfully, they didn't see Dad or Carrie again.

Despite Dad and the wind tunnel, it had been a lovely afternoon. When five o'clock came, Myra said goodbye to Shane.

"Text me, yeah?" He gave her his usual wink, a very quick hug, then he was gone.

When Mum arrived in the car, Myra had to explain

why her cap had changed colour. She said she had dropped it into the wind tunnel herself. Mum laughed.

"That was silly of you, wasn't it? How was Shona?"

"Who? Oh yeah, he's – she's fine."

She was praying Mum wouldn't talk to Dad. Not that there was anything wrong. But Myra knew from experience that other people never understood.

Lying on her bed that evening, she started texting Shane. There was a bit of a delay, then she got a message back, with all the hat or cap emojis that Shane could find. Myra texted back, with angry faces and faces with their tongues sticking out, and it all got very silly and a lot of fun.

Myra lay back on the pillow. She had the book open beside her, at page 47.

She had never enjoyed a day more…

She was worried every time the phone rang for the rest of the weekend, in case it was Dad. Why did she feel so guilty? She and Shane were just kids. They were only five years apart. There had been nine years' age difference between Granddad and Nan, and they had been together for forty years.

She didn't see Shane on the Monday morning bus, or during the day. Maybe he was off on another mission.

Then at afternoon break, she saw him at a corner table in the canteen. Two Year Eleven girls were talking to him, but then they went away, and Myra went and got a can of orangeade from the vending machine, the same as he'd had on Saturday, and took it to him. He smiled.

"Ah, aren't you good?" He opened it and took a swig.

Myra sat opposite him. Shane searched his blazer.

"Got something for you… hang on."

He turned out his pockets onto the tabletop. Myra saw his phone, another phone that was bright pink ("gotta return that"), a crumpled £5 note, black and blue leaky pens, a chewing gum wrapper, a strawberry bun that must have been in there since lunchtime, a 50p piece with the remains of a rubber band stuck to it, half a packet of Sweety-Breath mints, a small piece of igneous rock ("had that since first year, it's a kind of lucky charm"), two different sets of house keys and finally, very crumpled, very sat-on, her white cap.

"I went back there yesterday, got 'em to switch the current off. Got it back for you."

Myra gave him an *aww!* look. She could see the cap would never be the same again, but she could forgive Shane anything. She couldn't imagine schooldays without him.

Not for the first time, his phone went. Shane took the illegal call.

"Hello yeah? OK, I'll be there. After school."

He stuffed everything back into his pockets, leaving only the second set of keys, the strawberry bun and the cap. Then he took up the keys, jammed the cap onto Myra's head, stuck the bun into her astonished mouth, gave her a grin and vanished.

"*Mmmphff!* Shane!!!"

The next morning, Shane got on the bus from yet

another stop. He was looking very untidy and there was fluff all down his school trousers.

"Apols. I got ready in a hurry this morning."

"Oversleep, did we?" Myra smiled. She looked at his trouser-legs. "You look like one of those mummies in the Discovery Centre. What…?"

"I had to hide under someone's bed, last night."

Myra giggled. "No, come on. What really happened?"

They were growing closer and closer. They were texting each other every evening, meeting on the bus each day, and sometimes in school. If ever Myra had a bad time with the kids or teachers, she sent a quiet text to Shane that just said *Drama*. Then they met behind the Drama studio and had another hug. Every one left Myra feeling like her jet-propelled cap, going round and round…

Then on Thursday evening, almost a week after her trip to the Discovery Centre, Myra came in from school to find Mum sitting waiting for her at the kitchen table.

"Mum? I thought Nan was coming tonight?"

"I moved my shift," Mum said. She pointed to the chair opposite her. "Sit down."

Myra knew at once that something was wrong. She sat down.

"I spoke to your Dad on the phone, at lunchtime. About the Child Support. He told me he and Carrie met you in the Discovery Centre, at the weekend."

"Oh. Oh yeah. They did."

"With your friend. Shona?"

"Yeah."

"You liar! You were with a boy! A very big boy, Dad said! Almost a young man! *I'm sure you know all about it,* he said… smug little so-and-so!"

"So I was with a boy! He goes to school!"

"In what year?"

Myra paused. "Year Eleven."

"Year Eleven? He's nearly school-leaving age!"

"He's called Shane. I met him on the bus. He was nice to me…"

"Yeah, I bet he was! Didn't you think that was just a bit weird, Myra? A near-man, talking to a little girl like…"

"No, stop it! Just stop it! I know what you're saying, I know what you think he is and he's not, he's not a man yet, he's a boy, and he's been really kind to me and I know you think I'm stupid but I'm NOT and in that whole horrible school you sent me to, away from my friends, he's the only one, the *only* one who's been nice to me, instead of picking on me like Lara and Mr Barber and the boys and you and everyone else…"

She burst into tears and ran from the room.

Thirty-two seconds later, Mum heard her bedroom door slam and lock.

Myra flung herself on her bed, bucketing with tears. Then she lay there numbly, too exhausted even to message Shane. She wished he was here, to hug her.

He made everything feel better with his strength, his kindness, his funny jokes, and Mum wanted to take him and all that goodness away from her…

Then she made up her mind.

She went and fetched her rucksack, the big one she kept for holidays, and started stuffing items into it… clothes… her hairbrush… the book of fairy tales… and her crumpled white cap. Then she hid the rucksack inside the wardrobe.

Eventually Mum came and knocked, but Myra wouldn't come out. Finally Mum left her some supper on a tray outside the door. Myra took it in and ate it, as if on auto-pilot. She set an alarm on her phone.

The next morning she was up at 5.30 a.m. She washed and dressed and left the house before Mum was up. She was in school uniform, but was carrying the holiday rucksack in addition to her usual satchel.

She had a two-hour wait at the bus-stop before the school bus turned up. Luckily the weather was getting warmer now. There was hardly anyone around, apart from a few joggers and dog-walkers. A passing Jack Russell gave her a curious sniff, before its owner moved it on.

When the bus came, she went up to the top deck, but Shane wasn't there. No matter. He would be here, sooner or later.

She was starving with no breakfast inside her. She got in on the tail end of the Breakfast Club and got a slice of toast and a plastic cup of tea.

She went through the day as usual, doing lessons,

but not speaking to anyone. Lara tried a few jibes, but Myra wasn't even listening.

At the end of the day she went back and boarded the bus. She sat in their usual top seat, waiting for Shane.

Sure enough, just before the bus moved off, she felt his hands over her eyes. She smiled as he sat beside her.

"Hey. How was your day?"

Myra said nothing. Then she put her arms around him and gave him a great big hug. It was the first time they had done this with people around them. Year Elevens and Year Sevens were shouting and laughing and jeering, and John and Eddy were crowing at Shane, but Myra didn't listen to what they said. She didn't even notice Shane looking embarrassed. She didn't care about anyone or anything else, anymore.

Shane was rather silent after that. Outside the bus, the weather was worsening. The sky was growing darker and cloudier, and Myra could feel the electricity building up in the atmosphere. She could sense Shane beside her, and she felt alive.

When he got off at the first stop, Myra got off too. He looked puzzled, as the bus full of grinning kids moved off.

"Hang on. What's…?"

"I'm coming with you."

"What?"

"I want to see that secret life of yours. I'm never going back to Mum again."

"But Myra... you can't! I'm old enough to be your... brother!"

"I love you, Shane. And I want to be with you. Forever."

There was a flash of lightning, and the thunder rumbled. Myra felt the first drops of rain begin to fall. It was exciting. The first night of a new life. She could hardly even see Shane properly, or notice how wide and panicked his eyes had become. Myra was on page 47, and staying there.

"Do you love me, too?"

"Myra... calm down."

"Do you?"

"Well... yeah... but as a friend. As a *friend*, Myra. We can't be..."

"I'm not going to let you leave me, Shane! I'm not! I'm not!"

There was another flash of lightning. Myra ran forward.

Then she was in the road, with the car coming towards her. She saw headlights, heard the horn blare.

At the last second she felt Shane grab her arm, pull her back onto the pavement.

The car sped by...

Myra held onto him, her face wet with tears. The rain was falling heavily now. Both of them were getting soaked.

Like many a modern teenager, Shane never had a coat. He took his blazer off and held it over her.

"C'mon. I'm taking you home."

Myra stared at him. He had saved her, again…

They set off.

It was three miles home, and Shane walked her every step of the way. Myra didn't dare to speak, except to give directions. By the time they got there, her hair was plastered to her forehead, and Shane's brown face was glistening. The heavy rucksack on her back only made the journey harder. It was like some awful Army training exercise.

They staggered up the front path.

It was Nan who opened the door.

"What the heck's happened to you? Your Mum's been going frantic all day! She rang the school… but they said you'd been in…"

Shane caught his breath.

"She got off at the wrong stop, that's all. She's OK. I thought someone should walk her home."

"You must be Shane," Nan said. "You'd better come in."

Thankfully, Shane escorted Myra into the house.

Mum stood waiting in the hall.

She pointed at Myra, then at Shane.

"You… upstairs… hot shower… get changed. And you… young man… in here."

Looking genuinely afraid, Shane went into the kitchen.

Once she was warm and dry, Myra went slowly down and opened the kitchen door.

She found four mugs of hot tea, and Shane sitting

at the kitchen table with Mum and Nan. Shane's blazer was on the radiator, steaming quietly, and he was rubbing his hair with a towel.

To Myra's relief, Mum sounded calm.

"Shane's been telling me what happened in the street. I'd have thought you'd have more sense, Myra. If he hadn't been there…"

Myra bit her lip. "I'm sorry, Mum."

"Sounds like you've got a good friend here," said Nan. "Do you live far, Shane?"

Shane cradled the mug in his big hands. "Berwick Street. Just near the school."

"You can't go out again in this," said Nan. "You'd best wait 'til it's gone off."

In the end Shane had two slices of toast and a piece of Dundee cake, and another mug of tea, and they watched old comedies for three quarters of an hour. It was the first time Myra had brought anyone home from her new school.

Finally Shane's phone beeped and he muttered excuses and left, taking his dried-out blazer with him. He gave Myra a brief smile before closing the kitchen door.

They heard the front door slam.

Then Nan started to help clear the tea things away.

"He seems a nice lad."

"Mother!"

"Well, he does. Myra's lucky to have a nice big lad like that, to look after her. Just like me with your Dad. Remember why you're here, Julie."

"But Mother… he's sixteen!"

"So Myra's only got to wait a few years. Good fellas are hard to find. And he's nice-looking, too. I will be wanting great-grandchildren, you know…"

"Mother!!!"

Myra was teased about Shane for a few days at school, but things moved on. Lara and her friends were too busy with their hair and their reality shows and their messaging apps to worry about Myra for very long.

The weather grew warmer. Myra would soon be nearing the end of her first year. She knew she would never have got through it, without Shane.

They hadn't been out together again, but they still met on the bus, most days, and chatted. If anyone made fun of her, Myra remembered Shane's advice and talked back to them, or just glared them out. Then she was left alone.

Shane's conversation began to turn to the school Sports Day. He was doing PE for GCSE, and with his tall, athletic frame, he was expected to do well in the 400 metres and the Long Jump. He was now going for a run every morning before school. There were several trophies up for grabs.

Unusually, the Sports Day dawned warm and sunny. The whole school was allowed to wear sports kit for the day, and they all decamped to the Leisure Centre up the road, with its athletics track at the rear. The back of the Leisure Centre had a grandstand built onto it. Myra sneaked away from her form, and got a seat in the front row. She wasn't taking part in anything for hours, she was useless at sports anyway, and she wanted to watch Shane.

He was limbering up, the professional athlete. He was wearing the boys' P.E. kit of white T-shirt and shorts, showing off his tan.

The klaxon sounded, and the 400 metres began. Everyone was cheering someone on. Myra joined in.

"Come on, Shane! You can do it! Come on, Shane! Come on..."

She stopped, as she heard several other voices echoing the same words back at her.

She looked along the row. There were several other girls, on either side of her, and all of them were cheering Shane. They were all older than her, between Year Nine and Year Eleven, and those Shane's age were rather pretty.

They all sat in silence, and stared at one another.

When Shane won the race, none of them was even looking.

Myra had a few words to say to Shane that afternoon, when he staggered up to the top deck, laden with trophies and certificates.

He gave her a sheepish grin.

"So now you know my secret life. It's not my fault. I'm just good at looking after ladies. They need me, sometimes. I'm like one of them knights of old, riding out and rescuing damsons."

"Damsels."

"Well, OK. It's all quite innocent, mostly. It's like you and your fairy tales. Your Nan told me you like reading…"

"Shane! Shut up!"

"Well, you did ask me, that night. So I'll tell you. I love you all. In different ways."

Myra shook her head.

"Didn't know I was on a *list*. Now I understand those phone calls!"

"I'm always on duty."

"You're a funny boy, Shane."

"But you like me really, don't you?"

"Yeah. Don't know why!"

They were silent for a moment. The bus was quiet today. On a fine day, and in sports kit, many kids had walked it.

Then Shane said:

"You know I'm going soon? It's our Leavers' Assembly next week. Exams. Then…"

Myra's heart sank.

"We can still meet up, can't we… you know? Just friends."

"Oh yeah. Just friends. And you've got my number."

"Yeah, I have." Myra looked round. There was no one watching. She gave him another hug. "School's much better, now. Thanks for being my friend."

Shane laughed, and joined in the hug. The 400 metre trophy was digging into Myra.

Myra sat back in her seat. Then she remembered what Nan had said.

Shane was fiddling with his phone, as usual. Myra took hers from her satchel, and started to do the same.

She opened her calendar, flicked forward a few years, to when she would be leaving school too.

She started to make plans.

A Present from Owen

"If you think you're going to get that phone for Christmas now, you can forget it!"

The family car turned off the motorway. There was a small red and green stick-on sign on the rear window that said: *Merry Christmas*.

"It was only a joke," Owen said from the back seat. He held up a sign of his own he'd made when they stopped at a service station. It said: *Spot the turkey in this car*.

"I wondered what all those lorry drivers found so funny." Dad shook his head. "I've never been so embarrassed."

"Just trying to liven things up," Owen said. "While I still can. Before I have to spend another Christmas with the mad Aunt and Uncle. And share a room with Geeky Boy."

"Owen!" Mum put in, next to him. "That's no way to talk about your cousin."

"Wish *you* were a turkey," his elder sister Belinda put in, on Mum's other side. "I'd stick you in the oven."

Owen scowled. He looked out of the window at the choked traffic and the inflatable snowmen outside distant houses.

He hated spending Christmas away from home. This was the fourth year they'd all had to troop off to visit Aunt Julia and Uncle Gerry. And Cousin Crispin, who had an attic room that Owen would have to share.

Owen was getting ready for four days with no mates, and no telly.

"Television is such rubbish," Aunt Julia would say. "Especially at this time of year. We only keep one so Crispin can watch documentaries."

There wouldn't be any turkey, either. Aunt Julia and Uncle Gerry couldn't just have a normal Christmas lunch, like anyone else. Oh, no. They had to serve up a goose.

"*So* much more flavour," Aunt Julia said. "And more traditional. It was always a goose, you know, before we followed the Americans' example from Thanksgiving."

There certainly wouldn't be much Thanksgiving where Owen was concerned.

Owen hated goose, and the potatoes Aunt Julia roasted in the fat.

The car headed into the tree-lined streets where his aunt and uncle lived.

There was a loud snort as Grandma woke up in the front passenger seat.

"Nearly dropped off for a second there," she said. "What were all those lorry drivers hooting at, before? Was it something to do with Christmas?"

"Yeah, Grandma," Owen grinned. "That's right."

His grin faded as he saw the house looming up ahead. It was an old house, all twists and turns, and it made a point of being bigger than those around it. Like the people who lived there.

A sign on the gatepost read: THE GLEN.

The car stopped.

"Here we go again, then," Mum said. She took a deep breath. "Merry Christmas, everyone."

She followed Belinda out of the car. Owen decided to stay put as long as he could.

"*Welcome!*" Aunt Julia came rushing out into the street. She was wearing a skirt of purple velvet and a hand-woven shawl. And Uncle Gerry... Owen cringed.

Uncle Gerry had on a pair of illuminated antlers.

"Oh, darling!" Aunt Julia hugged Mum. "It's been too *long!*"

Owen thought it hadn't been long enough.

Very slowly, he forced himself to get out of his seat.

His best mate, Garth, was spending Christmas in Miami this year.

"Come on in, everyone!" Aunt Julia gushed into the house. "The holidays start here!"

The first thing Owen noticed was the smell of pine. There was an enormous Christmas tree, with lots of LED candles, and a model train filled with parcels, which a tiny Santa Claus was driving round and round the hall table. A huge golden banner across the hallway read GOODWILL TO ALL. Somewhere near, a very expensive speaker system was playing carols.

Owen sniffed. Aunt Julia didn't believe in doing things by halves.

"Come on, Owen." Uncle Gerry put on his best-mate voice as he led Owen forward. "Crispin's dying to see you. Come on, Crispin, say hello to your cousin."

"Hello," said Crispin. He was wearing a baggy jumper and an old pair of trousers, though his glasses did look as if he'd given them a polish for the occasion. He shook hands with Owen. "Season's Greetings, Owen. And a Happy New Year." He looked at Uncle Gerry, as if to say: *Will that do?*

"Hi," Owen said. He took another look at his cousin. Crispin was the thinnest boy Owen had ever seen. And one of the smallest. Though his head was huge, with those specs gleaming like headlamps. Maybe everything had been put into his brain.

"Crispin's got so much news to tell you, Owen," Uncle Gerry went on. There was silence. "Haven't you, Crispin?"

Crispin shrugged.

"I won the Chemistry Prize. For the whole of our region. And they're talking about putting me in for the national Maths test a year before everyone else."

"And his design for a wind farm," Uncle Gerry went on, "is being exhibited at the National Centre for Alternative Energy." He paused. "Are you still playing football, Owen?"

"Yes," Owen said.

"OK, everyone!" Aunt Julia stood on the bottom stair and clapped her hands for attention. "It's Julia and Gerry's Family Time! Now, here's the programme. One hour for settling in and general chat. Then, a Christmas

Eve glass of punch in the sitting room, before Julia's Three Fish Bake. Traditional parlour games after. Then, early to bed before Santa arrives! Tomorrow, there'll be the usual smoked salmon breakfast, with a glass of bubbly – just for the adults, sorry –"

No one laughed.

"And then," Aunt Julia finished. "There's a Santa hat for everyone, to wear to church."

She stepped over to Mum.

"By the way, Angela – presents. If you let me have them on the quiet, I'll finish making up the pillowcases before dinner. I've left a little bit of room for yours."

"This is your bed, this time," Crispin said. He showed Owen the bed nearest to the window in the attic room. "Hope you don't mind. The draught was bringing on my neuralgia."

Owen didn't even know what neuralgia was. He nodded.

He looked around the room. Most boys had posters on their walls of footballers or movies. Crispin had a star chart and the Periodic Table. There was a telescope beneath the skylight.

It didn't really matter what beds they had. This room was still cold. It might have been a bedroom to Crispin, but it still felt like an attic to Owen. To reach it, you had to take the stairs up from the hall, then another flight of stairs from a small, panelled area just off the first floor corridor.

Owen felt imprisoned, miles away from anyone. Except for Crispin. His cell-mate.

"Are you getting anything nice for Christmas?" Crispin asked. "I'm hoping for an oscilloscope."

"Dunno," Owen said. "Be a surprise, won't it?"

He didn't suppose he'd get that phone now. And if he did, he wouldn't be showing it to Crispin. Crispin would have the back off it in two minutes.

That was one thing about Aunt Julia's. Everyone got a pillowcase of presents to open, not just the kids. And Aunt Julia herself took them round, early on Christmas morning, before anyone was awake.

Owen grinned to himself. Maybe she couldn't get Santa to stop here.

He'd brought his Halloween pyjamas, especially for her. The ones with the fake blood on the shoulder.

"I'll let you unpack," Crispin said. "And then... how about a game of chess before dinner?"

Owen left the room without comment.

On his way downstairs, Owen stopped by Mum and Dad's room. They had the front bedroom. And Belinda – of course, *Belinda* got a room of her own, too.

He stood by the half-open door, and listened. Mum and Dad were talking in low voices as they unpacked.

"I don't know why we have to come every year, either," Mum was saying. "She was never that keen on spending time with me when we were kids. It was always the friends, from the Tennis Club, or college..."

"Family duty," Dad said. "It's expected, isn't it?

They come to us for Easter. So we come to them for Christmas."

"Oh, don't talk to me about Easter," Mum said. "I'll never forget what she said about my spring lamb. "Isn't it marvellous? How tasty these *Price Saver* things can be?""

"I had Gerry talking about his new car all weekend," Dad remembered.

"She's started already," Mum went on. ""Oh, I didn't think Gerry would be able to get the week off, he does work so hard now he's a *Senior Partner*. Have you seen this shawl? It was woven *especially* for me by an Andalucían lady we met...""

Dad laughed.

""And have I told you about Crispin?"" Mum continued the impression. ""He solved world hunger last holidays, and built his own medical research centre...""

Owen smiled to himself. He headed downstairs.

The family didn't know it. Yet. But this Christmas was going to be different. Owen was going to make it happen.

All he had to do was work out how.

"Found it!" Owen said. He produced the small, china thimble from behind the clock.

Crispin looked put out. "How did you know?"

Owen yawned. "You hid it there last year, too."

He looked back at the clock. It was still only ten past eight. Owen had drunk apple juice with Crispin while the others had their punch, and Aunt Julia's Three Fish Bake, with its floury, cheesy sauce, had made Owen long for fish fingers. The parlour games weren't up to much, either. The prize in Pass the Parcel had been a pencil sharpener, and as Belinda had refused to kiss anyone in the family, even on the cheek, Postman's Knock had been over quite quickly.

"When I was young," said Grandma from her corner chair, "every Christmas, we always used to make our own entertainment, like this. We'd play Hunt the Thimble, and Blind Man's Buff, and Forfeits. Then Father would lead the carol-singing." She sniffed. "It was incredibly boring. Can't we have the television on, now?"

"Sorry, Mother-in-law." Uncle Gerry beamed. "Telly's no go, in this house, come Christmas. It's People Time."

"We don't like Crispin watching it, anyway," Aunt Julia said. "It's incredible, the drivel they put on."

Owen felt a sudden, desperate urge to watch some drivel.

Then, an idea came to him.

"My turn, then," he said. He displayed the thimble. "Come on, Crispin, just you and me. While the grown-ups have a rest."

Mum and Dad tried to look as if this were how Owen normally behaved.

"That's a good boy," Aunt Julia said.

Owen moved to the door. "Give me two minutes, Crispin. And then come and find it!"

"Okay," Crispin said. He rolled up his sleeve and stood staring at his watch, timing to the second.

Owen rolled his eyes as he left the room.

Owen ran upstairs to the first floor, deliberately making all the noise he could. He moved along the corridor until he was just above the sitting room. There, he did a good deal of stamping on the floor, so Crispin would know where he was.

Then, he took his shoes off and crept back along the corridor to the attic stairs. That should keep Crispin quiet for a bit. And in Owen's rucksack, on his bed, were a handheld games console and a supply of sweets he'd brought to give himself a Happy Christmas.

Owen stopped.

The panelled wall, opposite the attic staircase, looked different from earlier.

It wasn't all wall. There was a door. And it was slightly ajar.

Owen pulled it open.

It was a cupboard. Inside, piled high, were several pillowcases, full of mysterious lumps and bumps.

He'd found the presents.

"Owen!" He heard Crispin's voice on the stairs from the hall. "Are you there?"

Quickly, Owen closed the cupboard and slipped upstairs to the attic room. He shut the door and switched the light on. He stretched out on his bed, pulling his fleece around him against the cold. From his rucksack he produced a family-sized chocolate bar.

Soon he heard Crispin below, at the far end of the corridor, hunting for the thimble. Owen took it from his pocket and grinned through a mouthful of milk chocolate. Crispin was in for a long search.

And he was in for a surprise, too. Finding the cupboard had given Owen another idea.

He'd worked out how to make this Christmas different.

Twenty minutes later, Owen heard footsteps on the attic stairs. He gave Crispin a grin as the door opened.

"I couldn't find it." Crispin had the look of annoyance of someone used to having the answer. "I looked in all the rooms. Where is it?"

Owen waved the thimble at him from the end of a finger. He laughed.

"Ah, cheer up." He took the last, tiniest fragment of chocolate from the packet. "Saved some for you."

Crispin didn't touch it. He went and sat on the end of his bed.

"You don't like me, do you, Owen?"

"Nope." Owen threw the thimble in the air and caught it.

"Why not?"

"Because." Owen sat up straight and looked Crispin in the eye. "Because you like Maths, and Science, and this room's more like a lab than a bedroom. Because you never stop going on about how clever you are, and neither does your Dad. Because you get spinach stuck in your teeth, and sniff all the time, and polish

your glasses with your sleeve and YOU'RE DOING IT
NOW! STOP IT!"

Crispin put his glasses back on.

"And," Owen finished. "I'm stuck up here with you,
every Christmas. While other lads are on the beach, or
watching TV."

Crispin said nothing. Very quietly, he left the room.

As soon as he'd gone, Owen pulled the Halloween
pyjamas from beneath his pillow. But he wouldn't be
going to sleep, just yet.

He had to stay awake, to carry out his plan.

Slowly, very cautiously, Owen reached out of bed. He
picked up his watch.

Twelve-thirty. Half an hour into Christmas Day. He
wished himself a Happy Christmas.

A shaft of moonlight through the skylight showed
Crispin, asleep. His glasses were on the bedside table
and seemed to be watching as Owen slipped from
beneath the bedclothes.

Owen caught his breath as Crispin moved in his
sleep, muttered.

Very carefully, watching Crispin the whole time,
Owen crept across to the door.

Owen switched on the pocket torch he'd brought from
home. He sneaked down the attic stairs.

Slowly, softly, he opened the cupboard door.

He lifted the pillowcases out carefully, one at a time,
like someone taking down a wall of sandbags.

He could tell who some of them were for, just from the colours. Bright pink would be for Belinda. A more tasteful pink would be for Grandma. The faded blue one, which looked like the oldest pillowcase of the lot, he was sure was his. And the selection box sticking out of the top proved it. Crispin would never be allowed that much chocolate.

He put the blue pillowcase to one side.

He'd have to work quickly. Any moment, Crispin might wake up, or one of the adults might come along the corridor to the loo.

He reached into the other pillowcases, one after another, and removed items, piling them high. Belinda's pillowcase was full of toiletries. Dad had shirts and aftershave. Uncle Gerry had cufflinks...

Owen started to mix everything up.

His hands moved fast. Presents flew past his gaze. Books. Sweets. Gift vouchers. Owen made them all into a great big stew on the carpet, before stuffing them back into different pillowcases.

A grin spread across his face as he shoved Crispin's *Young Person's Encyclopaedia of Knowledge* into Aunt Julia's case.

In two more minutes, all of the family's presents were thoroughly jumbled. Hardly anything was where it had started.

He'd time for a quick look at his own stuff. He pulled forward the blue pillowcase.

He dipped his hands in. Yes, this was him. Gel pens... handkerchiefs, euww. Some chocolate fudge.

A couple of quite good games for his console. And…
yes!

His grin returned as he saw the phone. There
it was, shiny, silver and high-tech, in its purple
presentation box, just like on the website. Good old
Mum and Dad!

He felt a bit guilty, at having included them in the
trick. Too late now.

He froze, as he heard a noise along the landing.
Remembering every spy movie he'd seen, Owen
flattened himself against the wall.

He knew, from the slow, measured footsteps that
made the floorboards creak, that it was Grandma. He
waited until he heard the bathroom door close after her.
Then he put his presents back in their pillowcase and
shoved all the pillowcases into the cupboard, taking
care to replace them in the same order.

He ran, as quietly as he could, back upstairs to bed.

Owen awoke. He blinked. It was daylight. A wintery
sun shone through the skylight.

He looked at his watch. Nine-twenty a.m.!

He looked across. There was no sign of Crispin,
whose bed was neatly made.

At the foot of Owen's bed lay the blue pillowcase.
Owen grabbed it and rummaged, pulling his presents
out. The pens… the games…

He frowned. He turned the pillowcase upside
down. Two tangerines rolled across the room.

Where was the phone?

He looked through everything again. No phone. No presentation box.

A distant sound came to his ears. Talking… no. Arguing. The occasional shout.

Owen grinned. He knew what that was about.

He pulled his dressing-gown around him and headed for the ground floor.

Owen pushed open the sitting room door.

"Morning, everyone. Happy Chr –"

He had to bite his lip to keep the smile from his face.

All around the room, the family were holding pillowcases and looking angry. Uncle Gerry was cowering by the piano from Aunt Julia, and the jolly Christmas hosts of the day before seemed to have disappeared. Belinda was crying, not upset-crying, the make-a-scene sort of crying that only teenagers can do.

"How old do you think I am?" She held up objects to show Mum and Dad. "A woolly cardie? Tights? *Anti-wrinkle cream?*"

"Really, Angela!" Grandma was sitting by the fireplace, looking miffed. "And you too, Julia. Is this how you see me?" She held up some thigh-high leather boots. "I'll never get my feet in there!"

"You only had to do mine!" Aunt Julia was yelling. "*One pillowcase*, out of all of them, Gerry! And what do I find! Encyclopaedias! A pass to the Museum of Physics! And then –!" She held up some gold earrings, in their box. "Do you think I'd wear awful common things like these?"

Next to the bookcase, Dad looked at Mum and mouthed: *I bought you those.*

Quietly, Owen left the room. His grin was growing too big to hide.

Mum's voice echoed along the hallway.

"Admit it, Julia! You always thought you were better than me! *Always*! Ever since you won the sewing prize when you were eight!"

Owen noticed there were no carols playing this morning. And the GOODWILL TO ALL banner was peeling off the wall.

Where was that phone? And where was Crispin? Owen had taken care to give him Grandma's *Tea-Room Guide to the United Kingdom*, and Mum's nail varnish.

He entered the dining room.

Crispin was there. Smoked salmon and scrambled eggs were already set out on the sideboard, with two bottles of bubbly. But no one had touched them. Crispin was sipping orange juice with his usual air of quiet superiority.

"Good morning, Owen," Crispin said. "And a Merry Christmas to you."

"You too," Owen smirked. "You were up early."

"I always am," Crispin said. "There's no point lying in bed. Do you know, if we used all the time we spend in bed for scientific research, we might have cured the common cold by now?" He looked at the clock. "It'll be time for church, soon. Where is everyone?"

"Opening their presents," Owen said. He still

couldn't keep his face straight. "Enjoy yours? I bet your Mum and Dad got you –"

He stopped, as Crispin picked up something from the table.

A shiny, silver phone, in a purple presentation case.

"Do you like my new phone?" Crispin displayed it proudly. "It's got all these new apps…"

"Hey!" Owen made a grab for it. His hand landed *slop!* in the butter. "That's mine! You stole it!"

"Yours?" Crispin grinned. Owen had never seen him smile before, let alone grin. "This is *mine*, from Mum and Dad. I found it in my pillowcase, this morning."

"Ah well, you're a liar, aren't you, Geek Boy?" Owen made another grab for the phone. "Because it wasn't in your pillowcase last night, when I –"

"When you what?" Crispin asked. Owen stopped.

Crispin reached for some toast and low-fat spread, avoiding Owen's hand in the butter dish. He added the spread to the toast with perfect neatness.

"A really strange thing happened last night. I got up to get a glass of water, and you weren't there. You know, you can see right to the bottom of the stairs, from the door of my room. So I went back to bed, waited 'til you came back, and then went down."

He took a bite of toast.

"Tell your Dad, or mine, if you want to. Of course, you'll have to explain how you knew what was in whose pillowcase."

He placed the phone out of sight beneath the table.

"I'll take this upstairs, afterwards. Who knows? If I take it to school next term, show it off, people like you might stop hitting me."

He raised his glass of juice.

"Merry Christmas. And thank you for my present."

Very slowly, Owen left the room and headed back to the staircase. He didn't feel he wanted any breakfast. Or Christmas goose, either.

In the hall, he paused by the Christmas tree, and looked upward.

The angel on the top seemed to be smiling.

Enjoyed this? Why not read…

THE ALIEN IN THE GARAGE AND OTHER STORIES
ROB KEELEY

Neil's little brother is driving him mad. There can't really be an alien living in the garage… can there?

Luke is bored. Adam has too much to do. Until they decide to swap lives…

A camping trip takes a spooky turn when a ghost story seems to be coming true…

These are just some of the tales in this funny and sometimes scary collection. You can also find out whether Liam and Justin would eat earwigs, why aliens like custard creams, and what exactly is the sinister creature lurking outside the tent…

*The Alien in the Garage and Other Storie*s will appeal to boys and girls aged 8-12… And parents reading the stories to their children! Written for those with a boundless imagination, a strong sense of humour and a desire to learn more about their world.

Available now from Matador in paperback and eBook

Enjoyed this? Why not read…

THE *(FAIRLY)* MAGIC SHOW AND OTHER STORIES
ROB KEELEY

Molly has just one day to become a magician...

There's someone very special in Mrs Hoskins' class. The question is – who?

A skipping rope holds the power of time travel...

These are just some of the tales in this second collection of funny, sometimes scary stories from Rob Keeley.

Available now from Matador in paperback and eBook

Enjoyed this? Why not read…

THE DINNER CLUB AND OTHER STORIES
ROB KEELEY

Longlisted for the International Rubery Book Award

Being on home dinners gives Aidan the chance to make some money…

A bridesmaid and a page chase a runaway wedding cake…

Mia and her Dad turn detective...

These are just some of the tales in Rob Keeley's third collection.

Available now from Matador in paperback and eBook

Enjoyed this? Why not read…

CHILDISH SPIRITS
ROB KEELEY

Longlisted for the Bath Children's Novel Award

"The truth will set you free."

When Ellie and her family move into Inchwood Manor, Ellie quickly discovers strange things are happening. Who is the mysterious boy at the window? What secrets lie within the abandoned nursery? Who is the woman who haunts Ellie's dreams – and why has she returned to the Manor, after more than a century?

Ellie finds herself entangled in a Victorian mystery of ghosts and tunnels and secret documents – and discovers that life all those years ago isn't so different from the world she knows today…

Rob Keeley's first novel for children brings out all the ingredients of the classic ghost story within a recognisable modern world setting. Readers of his short story collections for children will find in *Childish Spirits* the elements which made his past books such a success – strong and contemporary characters, inventive twists on traditional themes, and a winning combination of action, suspense and humour.

Available now from Matador in paperback and eBook

Enjoyed this? Why not read…

THE SWORD OF THE SPIRIT
ROB KEELEY

"There are truths which must be revealed before the battle may commence. You do not yet know the meaning of the sword."

Ellie's investigations into the spirit world have reached a medieval castle, where archaeologists are digging for the fabled Sword of St Merrell. But she didn't expect to meet a real medieval knight. Nor was she expecting him to be an ancestor of Edward Fitzberranger.

Ellie discovers that behind a legend of chivalry and bravery lies a dark and nasty truth. And worse is to come. Ellie's meddling has consequences she could never have foreseen. This time, she may have gone too far...

'… all the elements of a classic ghost story… but it also has a very modern setting… it's a breeze to read.'
Jill Murphy, The Bookbag on *Childish Spirits*

'... it's a terrific read, no matter how old you are! Chilling atmosphere, great sense of history, superb story all round.'
Books Monthly on *The Spirit of London*

Available now from Matador in paperback and eBook

Enjoyed this? Why not read…

HIGH SPIRITS
ROB KEELEY

Winner in Young Adult category of the Georgina Hawtrey-Woore Awards (formerly the Independent Author Book Awards)

"Millions of people will die in the war, Ellie. And it's our job to make sure it happens. That's why our work isn't easy."

The fourth instalment in the multi-award-listed Spirits series, which allows young people to learn more about other times, as well as the time in which they live.

High Spirits sees the series come of age and picks up with the central character, Ellie in her teenage years as she begins to realise the true nature of her abilities as one who talks to ghosts – and to discover her destiny. It sees her time-travel to the 1930s, as she discovers evil spirits and Nazi sympathisers working together in a way that will change the course of history. She then discovers the impact that such a change would have. It's a compelling ghostly thriller, which also allows some parallels to be drawn with the present day. It builds the ongoing story arc to a climax, which will be resolved in the fifth and final book of the series.

Available now from Matador in paperback and eBook

Enjoyed this? Why not read…

THE COMING OF
THE SPIRITS
ROB KEELEY

The Bookbag Top 10 Indie Books 2018

**"Nazis alone were dangerous enough, but Nazis
with the powers of ghosts... of evil spirits..."**

Britain. The present day. The world we know. Ruled by the Nazis.

Victorian England. Edward Fitzberranger is soon to become ill and die. But could there be another way?

The Middle Ages. Sir Francis Fitzberranger is about to marry... but finds himself shifted in time.

The barrier into the spirit world is finally breaking down and no one in the mortal world is safe. History must be set back on course and prophecies fulfilled. The Grand Defender is needed.

As Ellie works with an underground resistance movement and with the spirit world too, she is about to discover her true destiny...

Available now from Matador in paperback and eBook

Enjoyed this? Why not read...

THE TREASURE IN THE TOWER
ROB KEELEY

The Bookbag Top 10 Indie Books 2020

A school trip to historic Deanchester becomes more exciting when Jess and her friends discover the city hides a secret treasure. Local historian Dr Joseph Pyrite left a series of clues scattered around Deanchester's landmarks, which Jess, Mason and Kessie are determined to solve. But they only have three days. And they have competition. A series of increasingly cunning tricks awaits Jess and her party as they try to beat Perdita and Thomas to the treasure.

Available now from Matador in paperback and eBook